Home Sweet Home

A SWEET COVE, MASSACHUSETTS

COZY MYSTERY

BOOK 6

J.A. WHITING

To hear about new books and book sales, please sign up for my mailing list at: www.jawhitingbooks.com

For my family, with love

CHAPTER 1

A cake in the shape and colors of Mr. Finch's new house sat on a platter in the middle of the older man's dining room table. The four Roseland sisters and their boyfriends, Finch's girlfriend Betty Hayes, and Police Chief Martin and his wife Lucille crowded around and ooohed and aaahed over the magnificent sweet treat. Angie had spent hours creating the miniature replica of Finch's new home and her efforts were receiving high praise. Euclid, the Roseland's huge orange Maine Coon cat and Circe, their sweet black cat sat on the dining room side-table with their eyes glued to Finch as he attempted to cut the cake.

Mr. Finch was an adopted member of the Roseland sisters' family and his recently-purchased home was on a lot directly behind the girls' Victorian mansion. Raising his bushy gray eyebrows above the rims of his glasses, Finch held a knife suspended over the confection. He hesitated. "I can't do it, Miss Angie. It's just too beautiful."

Circe trilled encouragement while Euclid flicked

his enormous tail impatiently. He was hoping to get a lick of the cream cheese frosting.

"It's meant to be eaten." Angie urged the man. "Go ahead, cut it Mr. Finch. It's your favorite flavor and if we don't eat it, it will just go to waste." Angie was a professional baker and had owned a bake shop in the center of town until the lease ran out a few months ago. Now she created and delivered contracted treats to the restaurants and bakeries in Sweet Cove.

Finch's hand trembled as he held the knife poised over the roof of the house. He closed his eyes and gently pressed the sharp edge of the blade into the cake making the first cut. Everyone cheered. The aroma of cinnamon, nutmeg, and allspice floated on the air.

Betty Hayes put her hand on Finch's arm. "Would you like me to take over?" She batted her eyes at the man.

"Please." Finch, relieved, passed the knife to Betty and she sliced and placed pieces of cake onto plates.

Mr. Finch cut two small pieces from his slice and placed them on saucers which he set on the floor next to the side-table. "Here you are, my friends," he told the cats.

Angie's sister, Ellie, handed the plates around to the guests and everyone carried their treats into the living room where they sat and enjoyed the delicious carrot cake.

Tom opened a bottle of champagne and poured the bubbly into flutes. Jenna, Angie's twin sister, handed the glasses to the guests and when everyone had one, they raised them high in the air.

"Happy housewarming, Mr. Finch!" Twenty-two year old Courtney smiled broadly and clinked her glass against his champagne flute.

"Happy days and peaceful nights in your lovely new home." Ellie gave the gray-haired man a warm hug.

"At last, we get to celebrate your new house." Angie smiled and lifted a forkful of cake to her lips.

The Roseland sisters had been planning a house warming party for Mr. Finch for several weeks, but they'd all become so involved in solving a recent murder case that the festivities had to be postponed several times.

Jenna sat on the loveseat with Tom, his arm draped over her shoulders. "It's so great to have that case behind us and nothing to worry us now." She breathed a sigh of relief and reached over and gave Tom's hand a squeeze. The pretty diamond on her left ring finger sparkled in the light. Just a week ago, Jenna had accepted Tom's marriage proposal and since then, she'd been walking around like she was living on cloud nine.

Jenna's comment about having nothing to worry about because the recent case had been solved caused a skitter of unease to wash over Angie. Lately it seemed that as soon as one thing settled down something worse reared its ugly head demanding to be solved.

Finishing his cake and praising Angie for her efforts, Mr. Finch stood, leaned on his cane, and offered a tour of the house to those who hadn't yet seen it. The sisters' boyfriends followed after him to see the rest of the new place. Betty, a successful Realtor in the seacoast town of Sweet Cove, went along, too. She loved showing houses and she couldn't resist talking about the size of the rooms, the high ceilings, and the wood floors as if she might sell the home right out from under Mr. Finch.

Police Chief Martin's wife wanted to go along to see the house too, but before she joined the group in the foyer, she touched her husband's arm. "Ask them."

Carrying used plates from the dining room to the kitchen, Angie overheard Lucille's comment to the chief. She stacked the dishes next to the sink and turned around. Chief Martin stood in the doorway looking uneasy.

Angie cocked her head to one side causing her honey blonde hair to move softly over her shoulders. "What do you want to ask?"

The chief shuffled into the kitchen, making only brief eye contact. Jenna bustled into the room to get some cream from the refrigerator, but she stopped and stared at Chief Martin. She looked over at Angie. "What's wrong?"

"No one said anything is wrong." The chief shifted from foot to foot.

Jenna put her hands on her hips. "We know you well enough to see when something is bothering you."

"Tell." Angie stepped closer, a kind look on her face. "What do you need from us?"

The chief rubbed the side of his face and blew out a long sigh. "My aunt lives on the town line over by Silver Cove. She's older now, but she still has her faculties."

Silver Cove was a small town, a hamlet really, on the coast just north of Sweet Cove. It was a well-known artist colony and only had a population of about four thousand people even in the summer. Silver Cove had a rocky coast and just a few slips of tiny beaches here and there which kept the place from becoming popular with tourists. The section of Sweet Cove that abutted Silver Cove was very similar in its geography.

"Is your aunt having some kind of trouble?" Angie knew there must be a heap of trouble if the chief was so reticent about admitting what was going on.

Chief Martin swallowed hard. "She's complained about some odd things, strange noises, things being shifted around on the deck and in the yard. Sometimes, she thinks she hears someone walking around. She found a gray sweatshirt on the lawn the other day, didn't know how it got there.

5

She draped it over the deck railing thinking it might belong to the gardener. The next day it was gone and the gardener hadn't been there. There are other things."

"How long has this been going on?" Angie looked pensive.

"A couple of weeks."

"You want us to go see her? Check things out?" Jenna leaned back against the counter.

"I hate to ask. You're all so busy and we've had one thing after another to deal with here in Sweet Cove."

"We help each other." Angie smiled at the chief. "Ellie won't be able to come with us since she has to stay at the Victorian to handle the bed and breakfast, but Courtney might be off work tomorrow." Courtney and Mr. Finch co-owned a candy store in the middle of town.

Angie continued, "My new bake shop isn't ready to open yet and Jenna can have Ellie watch the jewelry shop while we drive over to see your aunt."

"It's only a ten-minute drive away." Jenna pushed her long brown hair over her shoulder. "We'll be back by lunchtime."

The chief looked like a weight had fallen from his shoulders. "I appreciate it." He managed a little smile.

"Want to go over some details until the house tour is over?" Angie whispered and gestured towards the upstairs. "Don't mention anything, ah, paranormal around the guys." Chief Martin knew not to talk about such things around anyone but family members, but Angie still felt the need to remind him.

"Only one of the men knows about certain skills that we have." Jenna winked. She had broken the news of the Roseland family's paranormal abilities to her boyfriend, now fiancé, and even though Tom had never heard anything like it, he was able to accept that not everything that's possible in the world is experienced with just the five senses.

"What do you think is the cause of what your aunt is experiencing?" Angie looked intently at the chief wondering if he had any insight.

Chief Martin rubbed the back of his neck and then shook his head. "I have no idea. She's getting older and maybe it's all just forgetfulness, but she's an intelligent woman and I tend to believe what she tells me."

"Tell us a little about her." Jenna glanced over the kitchen threshold to see if the other guests were still busy.

"Her name is Anna Lincoln. She's eighty-one years old. She lives alone in the family home where she grew up. It's a great house, right on the coast overlooking the ocean. Her husband passed away about twenty years ago."

"Does she have children?" Angie was taking it all in.

"She has a son and daughter. They live on the

West coast, both are medical doctors. Aunt Anna has a doctorate in biochemistry. She worked as a researcher and college professor for decades. She enjoys painting and quilting now, she even sells some of her work."

Since Angie had a degree in chemistry from MIT, she felt a sense of kinship towards the chief's aunt. "Your Aunt Anna was ahead of her time. She's such an accomplished woman."

"That's why I tend to believe what she tells me."

"Is she in good physical health? Can she manage in her house on her own?" Jenna asked.

"She does most everything on her own. She employs a gardener-handyman to mow and trim and he does odd jobs around the place. She cooks, walks to the market in good weather. In winter, her groceries are delivered."

"Does your aunt have social contacts, friends, a church group she belongs to?" Angie wondered if the woman kept to herself and didn't interact with others very much.

"Aunt Anna has a group of friends she meets in town for coffee pretty near every morning, mostly retired people. They range in age from their fifties to older than Anna."

Voices were heard as the tour group returned to the living room.

"You said that you're free tomorrow?" The chief looked hopeful. "I usually go see Anna every week and I'm due for a visit."

The girls agreed that tomorrow would work fine. Angie said, "I'll ask Courtney about joining us. Maybe she can come along."

"I'm sure she wouldn't miss it." Jenna chuckled. Twenty-two-year-old Courtney was the youngest Roseland sister and she loved mystery and intrigue. She and Mr. Finch loved to watch crime shows together and, after an episode, the two would spend time dissecting the perpetrator's actions and the detectives' handling of the case.

"I'll pick you up in the morning? After the early morning breakfast rush at the B and B?" Chief Martin suggested.

"We'll be ready." Jenna raised an eyebrow and smiled. "Shall we bring the cats?"

The chief spoke over his shoulder as he was exiting the kitchen, "That might not be a bad idea."

CHAPTER 2

Angie had been up since 4:30am to bake the bed and breakfast's morning goodies and the afternoon cookies and cakes. She wiped her hands on her apron and carried two trays of the treats to the kitchen's far counter. Ellie would place everything on attractive platters when it was time to serve them.

Ellie buzzed about the kitchen making waffles and scrambled eggs for her B and B guests. Courtney had already set out the different flavors of yogurt, filled the glass cereal containers, and placed the bowl of granola on the dining room buffet table.

She sat at the kitchen island spooning cereal into her mouth. "This visit to see Chief Martin's aunt is going to be interesting. He mustn't think that his aunt's worries are age-related. The chief must suspect something fishy is going up there otherwise he wouldn't ask us to come along."

"I guess we'll have to reserve judgment until we have a chance to talk to her." Jenna walked in wearing her pajamas and rubbing her eyes. She let out a wide yawn.

Courtney eyed her sister. "Good morning, sleeping beauty. I was about to come wake you. You don't want to miss a ride in Chief Martin's patrol car."

"It's too early," Jenna complained as she filled her mug with coffee. She was the only sister who didn't need to rise at the crack of dawn for her job. Her jewelry business was done mostly online so she could set her own hours to design and construct her necklaces, bracelets, and earrings. Customers visited her shop in the back of the Victorian, but Jenna didn't open the doors to clients until ten in the morning.

Ellie had worked in an assisted living facility for two years when she was in high school, so she had a bit of experience with the elder population. "People who are close to someone who is experiencing age issues sometimes dismiss the incidents because they don't want to admit that the person is declining." Ellie lifted the scrambled eggs from the pan into a serving dish. "It's very sad when someone begins to lose mental capabilities. It can be heart-wrenching for the relatives."

"Do you think Chief Martin is dismissing his aunt's complaints because he doesn't want to face the fact that such an intelligent woman is experiencing issues?" Angie finished her tea and placed the cup in the dishwasher.

"You'll have to figure that out when you visit."

Ellie removed a blue and white serving platter from the cabinet.

"Too bad you can't come along." Jenna buttered her toast.

"We'll consult with you when we get back." Courtney tilted her bowl to her lips to drink the remaining milk.

"Nice manners." Ellie scowled at her younger sister as she headed to the dining room with the scrambled eggs. Courtney ignored her. She'd heard Ellie's complaint about her cereal bowl manners about a thousand times.

"Where are the cats?" Jenna asked.

"They're on the porch waiting for Chief Martin." Courtney rinsed her dishes in the sink and placed them in the dishwasher. "I'm going upstairs to get my wallet. I'll meet you outside." She eyed Jenna. "You might want to speed it up."

Jenna was reading the news on her phone and chewing a bite of her toast. She batted at the air dismissively in reaction to her sister's comment.

On her way out of the kitchen, Angie said, "The chief is going to be here in five minutes."

Jenna's head snapped up and she squawked, "What? Oh my, gosh. I lost track of time." She nearly knocked Angie down when she tore past her in the hall on the way to the stairs and the shower.

***

JUST AS Jenna burst through the Victorian's front door onto the wraparound porch with her hair still wet from showering, Chief Martin's police car pulled into the driveway.

Euclid gave the tall brunette a scowl. He preferred punctuality.

Jenna gave him a look. "I forgot to set my alarm and the time got away from me."

Circe tilted her head towards Jenna so that she could get a cheek scratch and the young woman obliged by rubbing both of the cat's cheeks and the top of the feline's head.

Courtney was the first one off the porch. She greeted the chief with a warm smile. "I can't wait to meet your aunt. This is going to be interesting. Mr. Finch is manning the candy store this morning. He wants to hear all about our visit when we get back."

As the chief held the back door of the squad car open for Courtney, Euclid and Circe followed her to the vehicle and as they passed Chief Martin, he gave them a nod.

Courtney stepped back and let the cats into the car first and then she crawled in and took a seat.

Chief Martin smiled at Jenna and her dripping hair. "Too early for you?"

"Don't you start in on me, too." Jenna took a seat beside the cats who were sitting in the middle between her and Courtney.

"We're thinking of changing Jenna's name to Sleeping Beauty." Courtney chuckled.

13

Angie and the chief sat in the front of the squad car. Chief Martin backed out of the driveway and headed to Main Street where he took a right to drive north in the direction of Silver Cove.

"Does your aunt know there are six of us descending on her?" Angie watched the scenery as they drove along Main Street heading for the town line. Tourists were already out and about, some heading for the beach and others carrying take-out cups of coffee strolling along the sidewalks past the stores.

Chief Martin made a right turn. "I told her I was bringing all of you. I made up a story that the three of you have an interest in learning about quilting and would like to see some of her work."

"Does she know we have paranormal powers?" Courtney patted Euclid's head.

"I left that bit of information out of our conversation."

"Are we supposed to know that odd things have been happening?" Jenna asked. Circe was curled on the brunette's lap.

"I thought we could bring it up during our visit," the chief said. "I didn't want to make her think that I'd been talking about her to you."

Angie nodded. "That's probably a good idea. It can come up in conversation as we all chat. Hopefully she won't clam up about the subject because we're with you."

After a ten minute drive, Chief Martin turned the

patrol car onto a side street that ran off the main road between Sweet Cove and Silver Cove. They drove along the tree-lined lane past well-kept homes until the chief pulled into the driveway of a sprawling farmhouse with a wraparound porch.

"What a great house." Angie admired the beautiful property and smiled. "And it has a porch." She loved the homey feeling of sitting on a front porch with family and friends watching people strolling by.

As they piled out, Aunt Anna stepped from the front door onto the porch and waved. She was petite and slender with blond, chin-length hair. She was wearing jeans and a pale blue button-down shirt with the sleeves turned up.

She greeted the chief with a hug and a kiss and then turned to see Euclid and Circe walking towards her. "What lovely cats." Anna bent to scratch the animals' cheeks and was rewarded with purring. The woman seemed energetic and cheerful. When she straightened from patting the cats, she introduced herself, extended her hand, and shook with each Roseland sister. "Phillip tells me that the three of you are interested in learning about quilting."

For a half-second Angie hesitated wondering who Phillip was because the sisters only ever called the chief by his last name. "Yes, we saw some beautiful quilts at the Sweet Cove Fourth of July festival this year. One of the vendors was displaying some gorgeous handmade designs."

"Come into the house. We'll have something to drink and a bite to eat and then I'll show you my workroom."

The group entered the foyer which opened to a living area on one side and a dining room on the other. Wide, golden pine floors stretched across the space. The living room was decorated with cozy comfortable sofas and chairs and artwork hung on the walls. A huge bouquet of pink and white flowers sat in the middle of the old, oak dining table. There was a scent of cinnamon in the air.

"What a lovely home." Jenna's eyes were wide as she took in the cozy warmth of Anna's home.

"I grew up here." Anna led them into a huge country kitchen at the back of the house. The cabinetry had been painted a soft pale blue and a large table was placed in front of four windows that showed a nice view of lawn, flower and vegetable gardens. "I made some muffins." She gave Angie a little smile. "I understand that you're a fabulous baker. I was almost too intimidated to bake anything for your visit, but Phillip tells me that the three of you are lovely young ladies so I thought you'd be kind about my attempts to make some treats."

Courtney said, "Oh, don't worry. Your muffins smell delicious." She gave Anna a wink and a chuckle. "Anyway, Angie's stuff isn't all that great."

Angie elbowed her sister.

Anna laughed. "If you'll help me carry everything we can sit on the porch and have some tea and muffins." She looked down at the cats. "What can I give the kitties?"

Jenna lifted the two baskets from the counter, one with cinnamon raisin muffins and the other filled with blueberry muffins topped with cinnamon and sugar. "They'll be happy to have a bite of whatever we eat."

Everyone took seats at a round table on the porch and the cats jumped up on the railing to watch the proceedings. Anna poured tea and passed around small dessert plates and they each chose a muffin, or two.

A white van pulled into the driveway and parked on the far side.

"It's Jacob, my gardener and handyman."

A man in his thirties with dark brown hair dressed in jeans and a work shirt got out of the van and waved. He opened the doors at the back of his vehicle and removed two different sized clippers and a heavy rake and then he walked to the backyard.

Angie sipped from her China cup. "This is such a quiet, lovely street."

"Being here on the outskirts of town, we don't get the tourist crowds that you get in the main part of Sweet Cove," Anna said.

"Out here you must avoid the criminal element that sometimes comes with a huge influx of people." Jenna looked across the front yard at the Maple trees lining the street. "We've had our share of trouble in town recently."

"Oh, I know. It's such a shame." Anna shook her head. "But I think every place has its trouble in some form or another."

Courtney took the opportunity to ask a question. "Do you have problems out this way?"

Anna's hand showed a slight tremble as she set her cup on the table. "Nothing major."

Chief Martin cleared his throat. "Why don't you tell the girls about the things that have happened recently?"

Anna's face clouded and before she could say anything, Jenna looked at her with interest. She asked with a concerned tone, "What's been going on?"

"Oh, nothing important." Anna shook her head and narrowed her eyes at the chief.

Chief Martin decided to risk incurring his aunt's anger. "Some odd things have gone on recently." He listed the things he'd already told the sisters.

"There must be very good explanations for all of the little oddities. Maybe I'm just growing forgetful." Anna tried to dismiss the noises and items that had been moved or misplaced, but she couldn't keep a worried expression from showing on her face.

Before any of the sisters could ask further questions, the gardener, carrying a rake, rushed up to the front porch from behind the house. "Mrs. Lincoln." The man's face was creased with worry and his breathing was fast and choppy. His eyes were like saucers and he pointed to the farmhouse's backyard. "You need to see this. Down by the water." He gestured for them to follow him. "It isn't good."

CHAPTER 3

The people and animals hurried off the porch following after the man. Aunt Anna was surprisingly fit and quick. "What's wrong, Jacob?" she asked as she hurried along behind him.

"Down on the beach." Jacob pointed ahead to the path at the edge of Anna's property that led down the rocky coast to a slip of sandy beach.

Rushing along behind the others, Angie couldn't help but admire the seascape panorama that was visible from the back of the house. The farmhouse's lawn ended right at the edge of the rocks and the view of the sparkling ocean spread out before them.

When they reached the edge of the bluff, they stared down at a good-sized boat beached in the sand, listing to one side. Looking at the boat from high on the cliff, Angie's heart sank, worried that trouble had reached the outskirts of Sweet Cove and was about to fall into their laps once again.

"It washed up." Lines of concern were etched over Jacob's forehead. "Maybe it broke loose from its mooring. But maybe not." Everyone feared that the cause might be a man-overboard situation.

They all stared at the vessel for several moments. Courtney pulled her phone from her pocket and took a few pictures of the boat awkwardly perched on the slip of sand. Chief Martin blew out a breath. "Let's go check it out."

The group headed down the sandy path with the chief in the lead. Sea grasses grew on both sides of the dunes that nestled between the rocky cliffs. When they reached the tiny beach, Chief Martin called out for anyone aboard the boat. "Hello? Anyone there?"

There was no movement and no answer from inside the boat.

The chief called again and a woman's head popped up from below. She appeared disoriented, blinking in the bright sunshine. She lifted her hand to shade her eyes. Something about the woman caused jittery zings to jump over Angie's skin.

"Are you okay?" Chief Martin called to her and moved closer to the boat.

The woman ran her hand over her chin length auburn hair. A toddler's cry could be heard. The woman bent and scooped up a fussing child. She bounced him on her hip. "We're okay. We ran aground."

Courtney leaned towards Jenna and whispered, "Obviously."

"Can we help you down?" the chief asked.

"Let me just grab a few of our things." The

woman disappeared for a few minutes. When she reemerged, she had a tan backpack slung over her shoulder and her son in her arms.

Chief Martin moved aft to the metal ladder embedded in the side of the boat. He climbed halfway up and reached for the little boy. Clutching him in one arm, he took a few steps down and handed the child off to Aunt Anna.

The chief moved his feet back up the rungs and helped the woman onto the ladder. The two stepped slowly down to the sand. Circe scurried back towards the dune grasses and Euclid let out a low hiss.

"I'm Chief Martin." He extended his hand.

The woman shook hands with the chief. "Deirdre Collins." She reached for her toddler and bounced him in her arms. "This is Brendan." The woman's eyelids looked heavy and dark circles shaded the skin under her eyes. She was medium height and had a lean build like a long distance runner. Deirdre's eyes darted around and her movements were sort of twitchy giving the impression that she was a bundle of nerves. Angie estimated that she must be in her early thirties. The Roseland sisters and the two cats watched the woman carefully.

"Is there anyone else in the boat?" the chief asked.

"What? No." Deirdre rubbed the child's back. "Where are we?"

"This is Sweet Cove," the chief told her.

"Although, we're right near the town line with Silver Cove. I'd like to ask you a few questions, if I may."

Deirdre gave the chief a brief look as if she didn't know what he was saying, but then her face cleared and she nodded. "Why aren't you in uniform?"

"I'm off duty."

Aunt Anna stepped forward. "Shall we go up to the house instead of standing in the hot sun? Have a cold drink while you talk?"

Chief Martin gestured to the path. "Good idea."

The group started up the hill to Anna's farmhouse with Anna and her gardener leading the way, followed by Deirdre and her baby. Before falling into line, Euclid eyed the three Roseland sisters and let out a hiss.

Chief Martin looked at the orange cat and said quietly, "I agree."

Deirdre climbed the hill after Anna. Chief Martin offered to carry the toddler up to the top, but Deirdre told him it was no trouble for her to manage.

When the group was walking across the grass to the house, Deirdre asked, "Where's my husband?"

Chief Martin halted with a surprised look on his face. "Your husband?"

Deirdre turned. "Isn't that why you're here? Didn't he contact you about the boat?"

The Roselands exchanged quick looks with one another.

"What do you mean, ma'am?" The chief narrowed his eyes.

"Didn't he call you? About the boat? That we were grounded?" Deirdre's voice was insistent.

"We just happened to see you from the bluff." The chief's face was serious.

Deirdre stopped and blinked. "Well, where's Tony?"

"Let's go to the house and we'll clear everything up." Chief Martin gestured to the front porch and they crossed the lawn to the farmhouse.

Courtney whispered to her sisters. "Something isn't right here. She seems off." Angie and Jenna nodded. They'd each been thinking the very same thing.

Once they reached the house, the group settled on the porch chairs and Anna hurried off to the kitchen to get some juice for the little boy and a coffee for the young mother. Angie watched the woman closely trying to get some sense of her. Deirdre seemed distracted and unfocused and even though her outward appearance suggested fitness and strength, her demeanor gave the impression of frailty.

Before the chief took a seat, he had given the Roseland sisters a nod and a raised eyebrow indicating that he wanted their help in the questioning. Angie assumed that the chief was getting the same impression of the woman that she and her sisters shared.

"Can you tell me how you managed to get grounded here?"

Puzzlement showed on the woman's face so the chief asked a different question. "Where do you moor your boat?"

"In Sweet Cove harbor."

"How long have you been in Sweet Cove?"

"Almost a month. We usually keep the boat in Oak Bluffs on Martha's Vineyard. We wanted a change."

"Was your husband on the boat with you?" the chief asked.

Deirdre nodded her head vigorously. "Of course he was."

"He isn't in the cabin right now?"

"No." The woman's voice was becoming higher-pitched.

The chief stood up. "Were you traveling during the night?" His voice had taken on a tone of authority. He pulled his phone from his back pocket.

"Yes." Deirdre held her son in her arms. "Do you know where Tony is?"

"Where did you leave from? Sweet Cove harbor?"

"No. We were on Marion Island." The island was about fifty miles off the coast of Massachusetts and many wealthy individuals had vacation homes there.

Angie leaned forward. "What time did you leave

the island?"

"I'm really not sure, maybe around midnight?" Deirdre gently rocked her sleepy son. "Is Tony coming to pick us up?"

"Have you called your husband? Does he have a cell phone?" Jenna asked.

"He left it on the boat."

"When did he leave the boat?" Chief Martin asked.

"I don't know." Deirdre looked away.

"How do you *not* know when your husband left the boat?" Courtney scowled. "The boat isn't that big."

"Brendan and I were asleep in the cabin." Deirdre's mouth turned down and she sat back in her chair taking on a defensive posture.

"Where did your husband go?" Jenna's blue eyes narrowed.

"I thought he left to get help or to go get the car." The toddler squirmed out of his mother's arms and sat down on the porch to watch the cats. Euclid gave the little boy a warning look, but Circe allowed the child to stroke her fur.

"Where do you keep the car?" the chief questioned.

"Either at the harbor lot or in the driveway of our studio apartment."

"And what is the make and model? And the color of your vehicle?"

Deirdre told him.

The chief asked where the family was living and the young woman gave the address of their studio apartment in Sweet Cove.

Angie asked. "Did your husband tell you he was leaving the boat?"

Deirdre shook her head.

"You just assumed he went to get help?" Angie's heart started beating faster. She couldn't understand what had happened on the vessel. "When was the last time you talked to your husband?"

"Right before I went below to sleep."

The chief excused himself and walked down onto the lawn to make the emergency call to the Coast Guard to report a possible man overboard. Then he made two other calls, one to the Sweet Cove Harbor Master to report the grounded vessel and the other to the police station. "I'm going back to the boat to check it out."

Courtney blew out an exasperated breath. "I'm not clear about what happened to you and your husband last night."

Deirdre repeated what she'd already told them. Anna brought out some muffins and offered them to the guests. There was some awkward chit chat, but mostly everyone sat quietly sipping their drinks.

Chief Martin returned to the porch and sat down. "The boat is all clear." He asked Anna for a piece of paper and a pen. She went inside and quickly returned with the items. The chief looked at Deirdre and asked gently, "Will you recount the events of the evening for us, please?"

"We went to Marion Island for the day. Last night, we started back to Sweet Cove around midnight. I was in the cabin with Brendan and we fell asleep. I had a migraine starting and sleep always helps."

"Did you see your husband again during the night?" Angie asked.

Deirdre shook her head. "Something woke me sometime around 2am. I called for Tony but he didn't answer. I thought the engine noise probably kept him from hearing me."

"Then what happened?" Courtney did not like this woman.

"I fell back to sleep until around 5am. I woke up to find that the boat was grounded. We were listing to the side. I got out of bed and went up to the deck. Tony was gone. I assumed he'd gone to get help."

"What did you do next?" Jenna asked.

"I went back to the cabin and went back to sleep." Deirdre turned to the chief. "I woke up when you called out."

Courtney narrowed her eyes and the muscle near her jaw gave the tiniest twitch. "So you got on the boat and then you didn't see your husband again during the next ten hours." She was incredulous.

Deirdre lips tightened defensively. She didn't

28

say anything to Courtney's observation.

Did you or your husband drink any alcohol last night?" Angie asked.

Deirdre shook her head. "No. Well, just a glass of wine. Tony doesn't drink a lot when he mans the boat."

"What about you? Did you have a nightcap?" Jenna pressed.

"Just a half glass of wine. My head felt funny all day. I was pretty sure a migraine was on the way." Deirdre moved her index finger to her temple and rubbed.

After twenty more minutes of questioning and discussion, a police car drove up to Aunt Anna's house and Officer Talbot got out and approached the porch. He nodded to everyone and made eye contact with Chief Martin who excused himself and stepped to the lawn to speak with his officer. A shiver of worry slid down Angie's back. She shared quick looks of concern with her sisters.

Chief Martin approached the porch. "Mrs. Collins. Your car is still parked in the harbor lot. There isn't any sign of your husband down at the harbor and one of our officers knocked at your apartment door and no one answered. If you don't mind, would you please come with me down to the station?"

Deirdre stood up with a start. "Where's Tony then? Why do I need to come to the station?"

"We can talk more about last night's events and

29

we'll organize a search for your husband." The chief's expression was solemn. He went up to the porch to gather his things and to give Aunt Anna a goodbye hug.

Deirdre's eyes went wide. She started to bluster something, but stopped. She picked up her son and followed the chief to his car, her gait a bit awkward and unbalanced.

Chief Martin turned to the Roseland sisters. "Officer Talbot will drive you home. I'll be in contact." He gave the girls a pointed look which told them that their skills might be needed on the case.

Angie stood up and said to Anna. "I'm sorry our visit was so short."

"Come back any time." Anna gave each of the girls a hug. "I hope this gets resolved quickly and the poor young woman's husband is found safe and sound."

While Jenna nodded and thanked Anna, she knew deep down that there was trouble ahead.

Courtney and her sisters helped clear the table and brought the dishes and cups into the kitchen. "This whole mess is one of the weirdest things I've heard. It sounds like something that should be on one of the crime shows I watch with Mr. Finch."

As the girls climbed into Officer Talbot's cruiser, Angie thought that Courtney was probably right on target and her heart sank.

CHAPTER 4

Mr. Finch was at the dining room table eating his lunch when the three girls and two cats walked into the foyer. "Well, how did it go? What did you learn?"

Ellie came into the room carrying a bowl of roasted tomato soup. "You're back." She sat down next to Finch. "Did you figure out what was happening with the chief's aunt?"

The girls took seats on the other side of the table, but no one said anything. The cats jumped up on top of the China cabinet.

"I can see that things did not go well." Finch put down his spoon and waited to hear what had happened.

"We didn't have a chance to get into Aunt Anna's concerns or worries," Jenna said. "Something else came up."

The three sisters took turns telling about their morning with Aunt Anna and the strangeness of the circumstances of the grounded boat.

Courtney said, "That woman has guilty written

31

all over her. How is it possible to wake up, discover that your husband is missing, and then go back to sleep? They had been out in open water. The boat was grounded. Does the thought that your husband might have fallen overboard not enter your mind?" Courtney got up shaking her head. She moved around the table and sat down next to Mr. Finch. "Are you going to finish that soup?"

The older man slid the bowl in front of the honey blonde.

Ellie's face scrunched up. "How terrible if the poor man fell into the ocean. So many hours passed before help was called."

"What do you think?" Finch eyed the girls. "What do you sense? Did the man get off the boat and go for help?"

Euclid let out a long, low hiss.

"It's possible." Jenna pushed her hair away from her face. "But maybe not probable."

"Miss Angie?" Finch made eye contact with the older sister.

Angie sighed and shook her head. "I think we're going to be drawn into this. I think Chief Martin will be looking for our help. I'm not sure what's happened to Tony Collins."

"What about the woman? Mrs. Collins." Ellie's face was serious. "Do you get a feeling one way or the other about her guilt or innocence? Courtney seems to be leaning towards guilty."

Jenna shrugged and shook her head. "It's too

32

soon to say."

Angie pushed her hair behind her ear. "We didn't have enough time with her. We were trying to figure out what happened. It was odd the way Deirdre didn't seem to be alarmed when she woke up and her husband wasn't on the boat. I was sort of baffled by her response. I wasn't paying any attention to psychic signals."

Finch looked at Courtney. "Is your suspicion of her a result of a *feeling* you were getting from the woman?"

Courtney used a napkin to wipe a drop of soup from her chin. "It was because her answers seemed ridiculous."

"The woman said that she and her family had gone to Marion Island for the day." Mr. Finch reviewed what was known. "They were returning to Sweet Cove last night. She and her son went below deck to sleep and Mr. Collins was at the helm."

Jenna nodded. "That's what she said."

"I wonder," Angie pondered, "if they'd made the trip before. I wonder if Mr. Collins was experienced boating in the dark."

"And what about the sea conditions?" Jenna sat up. "Maybe there was something unexpected during the trip. Large waves? Maybe a wave hit the boat and Mr. Collins lost his balance and went over the rail." She shrugged a shoulder. "We're not sailors so we don't know if that's possible."

"Maybe this whole thing was an accident then."

Ellie reached for a freshly-baked roll from the basket in the center of the table. "Maybe there is no foul play at all."

Courtney gave Ellie a look. "Maybe not," she said reluctantly, but then added, "I think Mrs. Collins knows more than she's saying."

"Hopefully the man shows up unhurt." Angie glanced up at the cats and saw that Euclid was scowling at her so she voiced another thought. "At least we can hope that it wasn't murder. Maybe we'll find out that it was an unfortunate accident." She gave a sigh. "We'll need to return to Aunt Anna's place one of these days to see about the noises she's been hearing. At dinner, we should talk about when all of us can go back to see her."

Jenna looked from Mr. Finch to Ellie. "Maybe you two should come with us when we return. You can meet Anna and then we can show you where the boat washed up. You might be able to sense something."

Ellie's eyes widened and then she made an excuse. "I'll probably need to stay here for the B and B guests." Ellie preferred to keep as far away from trouble as she could and she encouraged her sisters to look into things without her. The others understood that Ellie's reluctance was based on fear of the unknown and a strong aversion to hearing about crime and cruelty.

"I'd be glad to come along the next time you visit Ms. Anna," Mr. Finch said.

34

Courtney got up and headed for the kitchen carrying the empty soup bowl. "I'm going to the candy store now. I'll see everyone at dinner."

Courtney and Mr. Finch were taking turns managing the store. They were trying to keep Finch's hours to a minimum since he'd suffered a blow to his head a few weeks ago during the last murder case he and the Roseland sisters had been involved in solving.

When Courtney was gone, Mr. Finch spoke. "My candy store partner seems to hold a strong belief that Mrs. Collins is not being upfront about what happened on the boat."

Angie narrowed her eyes. "Courtney isn't usually so quick to judge."

"Perhaps there's a reason for her reaction." Finch pushed his chair back and took hold of his cane which had been hooked over the edge of the table. "I'm going to head home and take a quick nap. Call me if you need me."

Circe jumped down from the China cabinet and followed the older man down the hall and out the back door. Since his injury, the lovely black cat had taken on the job of watching over Finch and she often went home with him when he needed to rest. Mr. Finch had hired a mason to build a stone walkway through the small thicket of trees from the back of his house to the Roseland's yard. It was only a short stroll to go from one house to the other.

Jenna yawned.

35

"Did you get up too early?" Angie teased.

Jenna ignored the comment. "I'd better get to work on some jewelry. If Chief Martin needs our help, I don't want to fall behind on production. I need to get some pieces out to customers soon." She stood and started for her shop at the back of the house.

Angie said, "I need to go over the equipment orders for the bake shop. Supposedly the new refrigerator is on back order so I need to deal with that." Now that the renovations were nearly complete, Angie was planning on re-opening her Sweet Dreams Bake Shop very soon and there were many organizational tasks that she had to see to.

Ellie looked up from her bowl. "There's soup in the crock pot if you're hungry. You'd better eat because I bet that very soon Chief Martin will be calling on all of you to help him."

As soon as Ellie finished her statement, Angie's phone buzzed. She looked down at the screen and then raised her eyes to Ellie. "It's Chief Martin."

CHAPTER 5

Angie took the call from the chief in the living room. She clicked off and walked through the foyer into the dining room. Ellie was wiping off the dining room table with a white cloth and she looked up when Angie came back in.

"How did you know Chief Martin was going to call?" Angie eyed her sister.

"It wasn't hard to deduce that he would be in touch with you." Ellie continued her task.

"But you said he would call the very moment before my phone buzzed. Did you sense the incoming call? Could you tell he was making a call to me?"

Ellie's long blonde hair fell forward over her shoulder and she pushed it back. She smiled. "Not everything is paranormal activity, you know."

"I just wondered if you were developing new powers," Angie said.

Jenna was standing by the hallway entrance. She shrugged a shoulder when Angie made eye contact with her. "What did the chief say?"

37

"Tony Collins is still unaccounted for. Mrs. Collins spoke with the chief at the station, but nothing new was revealed and she and her son were driven home. The Coast Guard has a search underway and is meeting the chief at the boat to conduct an investigation." Angie started for the hallway that led to the kitchen. "The chief wants us to ask around town, see what we can find out about Tony Collins. He'd like us to meet with Mrs. Collins later this afternoon. See if we can get any more information out of her. Will you come along?"

"Of course," Jenna said. "I'll go change. Are we leaving now?"

Angie walked down the hall. "First I need some soup."

***

JENNA AND Angie headed down Main Street to Coveside and the Sweet Cove harbor. They'd eaten lunch and cleaned up and discussed the case and the investigation. Euclid had perched on top of the refrigerator listening to the girls talk. They wondered about Deirdre Collins' unexpected behavior and why Tony would leave the boat looking for help without telling his wife he was leaving. So many things seemed off.

Jenna had said, "But a lot of people are strange and do things differently than we would. It isn't indicative of a crime." The expression on her face looked like she was trying to convince herself that a crime hadn't been committed, but it didn't seem that she believed her statement.

Euclid didn't either. He hissed whenever the girls proposed the possibility that Tony Collins had just wandered off or that he was knocked from the boat by accident. Angie made eye contact with the huge orange cat and said gently, "Not everything is a crime, you know." Euclid hissed again.

The Sweet Cove harbor was a small natural inlet that sheltered sailboats and powerboats. A pedestrian drawbridge spanned the narrowest part of the harbor and linked the tourist area of Coveside to the more residential section on the other side of the harbor called South Coveside.

Angie and Jenna walked along the brick sidewalks past gift shops, restaurants, and coffee shops. Flowers overflowed from window boxes and stoneware pots that had been placed at store entrances, and colorful blooms filled well-tended small garden plots next to restaurants and shops. Park benches and chairs stood here and there throughout the area and lined the walkway that meandered next to the harbor.

The girls decided that their first stop should be the small coffee shop tucked at the end of one of the cobblestone lanes where locals and fishermen hung out. A bell tinkled when the door opened and it reminded Angie of the little bells that used to chime when the door to her bake shop opened. She couldn't wait to re-open her café and have all of her old customers return and enjoy the new store.

The little coffee shop in the cove was packed with workers and fisherfolk eating late lunches or having coffee and pastry. Angie and Jenna took seats at the breakfast bar and the young woman behind the counter recognized them from town and came over to take their orders.

"Hey," Louisa said. "Haven't seen you around much." She had her long black hair pulled back into a ponytail. The ends of her hair were tinted with blue highlights and her bright blue eyes stood out against her tanned skin.

"We've been busy with different projects," Angie told her. She left out the fact that the projects had been murder cases.

"How are things with you?" Jenna asked.

"I'm good." Louisa looked around the café. "It's super busy today."

"How come?" Jenna tilted her head in a questioning posture. "Anything going on?" She hoped people had gathered to share and hear gossip about Tony Collins and his disappearance.

Louisa nodded. "Have you heard about the guy who went missing today? He had a boat moored down here."

Angie wanted to hug the girl for bringing up the very topic they wanted to discuss. "We were up near Silver Cove this morning visiting someone. We actually saw the grounded boat. What's the news?"

"The Coast Guard is doing a search with boats, a plane, and a helicopter and the police are searching the town and surrounding area looking for him." Louisa leaned close. "They wonder if he might have smacked his head, maybe has some amnesia or something and is wandering around, confused."

Jenna's eyes widened. "Really? Why do they think that? Did they get a tip from someone?"

The pretty young woman shook her head. "I think they're just hopeful that he's alive and that amnesia would explain why he hasn't gone home or called the harbor master about the grounded boat." Louisa eyed Jenna's engagement ring. "I heard the good news." She smiled. "Congratulations." She went to get the girls their cups of tea.

"Amnesia, huh?" Jenna looked doubtful.

"I guess they have to cover all the bases." Angie glanced around the room at the groups of customers chatting with one another. She kept her voice down. "I wonder if someone in here has some useful information."

"The problem is finding out *who* knows anything that could help."

Louisa returned and set down two steaming mugs. There was a lull in the action so she leaned against the counter. "Did you hear the wife and child were on the boat?"

The girls nodded.

Louisa shook her head and let out a sigh. "Poor

guy. He used to come in here. Get coffee, a donut. He'd talk with the regulars. Hard to believe he might be dead."

"Did he chat with anyone in particular?" Angie asked.

"Whoever happened to be in here at the time." Louisa looked around the room and tapped her finger on her chin. "You know, there was something about him."

Angie and Jenna waited for the waitress to elaborate. Just when Jenna was going to ask for details, Louisa said, "He was always friendly, but was kind of arrogant, cocky. I don't know, there seemed to be some kind of weariness about him, like he always needed action or excitement or something new."

"Did Collins talk to you?" Angie sipped her tea.

"Yeah. Nothing deep or anything, just general chit chat."

"Did he say why he was in Sweet Cove?"

"Tony said he was an investor, had a few businesses. He liked to be his own boss. He mentioned some land development deal, building homes over on Marion Island. He complained about his partner, but I really didn't follow what his gripe was. Tony liked the North Shore coast and he thought he could do land development around here, too."

"Did his wife ever come in?"

"I didn't even know he was married." She

scowled. "Never even heard him mention his wife or his kid. Which seems kind of strange, doesn't it? Most people talk about their kids." Louisa shifted her feet and made eye contact with the sisters. "When he'd come in, Tony would flirt with me. He was a nice looking guy. I enjoyed it." She rolled her eyes. "I have to say I was pretty surprised when I heard he was married." Louisa harrumphed. "It's not the first time that's happened and I'm sure it won't be the last."

Angie gave her a sympathetic look. "Do you know where the Collinses came from?"

Louisa thought for a few moments. "I don't know. I don't think I ever heard."

"What do people think happened on the boat?" Jenna asked. "Have you heard conversations?"

Louisa made face. "No one knows. There are plenty of opinions, but that's all they are, guesses, hunches, ideas. Some people think he fell off the boat, others think the wife pushed him."

"Did Tony have any enemies?" Angie asked. "Did he have any run-ins with anybody?"

"Nothing I knew of," Louisa said. "He hadn't lived here that long."

A group of people entered the coffee shop and as Louisa went to seat them, she gave the girls a smile. "Nice to see you two. Don't be strangers."

Angie and Jenna finished their tea and stepped outside.

"That wasn't that helpful," Jenna noted.

43

"We learned some things though." Angie turned onto a side street. "Collins was arrogant, seemed to need excitement." She held up a finger for each point covered. "And he never mentioned his wife."

"Or his kid." Jenna added.

"He flirted with pretty girls."

"Well, one anyway," Jenna said.

Angie turned down onto a side street.

"Where to now, Sherlock?" Jenna kidded.

"Time for a visit." Angie led the way to the pedestrian footbridge, but then she stopped. "I think we should make a detour before we head over to see Mrs. Collins." She turned back to the main thoroughfare and entered the small toy store where she bought a stuffed dinosaur. The girls' next stop was to the gift shop on the corner. They picked out a porcelain tea cup, a variety of different flavored tea bags, and some English biscuits which the clerk wrapped in tissue paper and placed in a pretty gift bag.

Angie and Jenna carried the items over the footbridge and walked several blocks past nicely tended single family homes. Angie checked the text message from Chief Martin indicating the Collins's address. "It's the next house. The garage in back has been made into an apartment."

Walking down the driveway, they could see that the front door of the little place was open. Just as Jenna knocked on the doorframe, the sounds of crying could be heard inside. The girls exchanged

44

looks and Angie poked her head in. The space had been made into a studio apartment with a sofa and a chair at the far side, a kitchenette along the left side wall, and a small table and two chairs placed in front of a window. There was a portable crib tucked into the corner near the sofa. Mrs. Collins sat on the couch, sniffling and dabbing at her eyes with a tissue.

"Deirdre?"

The woman looked up, startled. As she blinked and wiped the tears from her cheeks, Deirdre recognized Angie. "Oh." She stood up.

"We thought we'd stop by. See how you're doing." Angie stepped into the room with Jenna right behind her. She was surprised that the family was only renting a studio sized apartment. It didn't seem large enough for two adults and a toddler.

Jenna moved forward and gave the young woman a hug. "We brought you something. And this is for Brendan." She handed Deirdre the gift bags.

Deirdre scrunched the tissue in her hand and a flood of tears cascaded over her cheeks. "I'm doing terrible. Everything is terrible." Her voice squeaked.

Jenna placed her arm around the sobbing woman's shoulders.

Angie wondered if Deirdre had just received bad news about her husband. "Are there any updates from the police?"

Deirdre shook her head and practically wailed. "I'm being kicked out of here." Her hand flapped in the air gesturing about the room. "Where am I going to go? I don't have any money. I have to get out today, in a couple of hours."

Angie asked, "Why do you have to get out?"

Jenna steered the woman to the tiny wood table and had her sit in one of the chairs. Jenna sat opposite. "What's going on?"

Angie pulled a director's chair over. "Why do you need to get out today?"

"The landlady said Tony only rented the studio for the month. She has new people scheduled to arrive this afternoon. This is just a short term rental apartment for tourists." Her lip stuck out in a pout. "I thought we had the place 'til the end of the summer. I can't handle a toddler on a boat. That's why Tony rented us this place. It's safer here for a toddler than on a boat. Brendan is just starting to take some steps, but soon he'll be running all over. I'm always afraid he'll fall off the boat. "

The little boy stirred from sleep in his portable crib.

"I don't know what I'm going to do." Deirdre pushed her hair back from her face. Dark circles showed on the pale skin under her eyes. Her face looked gaunt and her shoulders drooped.

"Could you rig up some baby gates or some kind of fencing on the boat deck?" Jenna asked.

Deirdre shook her head. "The boat is in police custody right now. So is our car. I'm not sure when they will be released to us. I don't want to live on that boat anyway."

Angie thought it was odd that Deirdre hadn't uttered one word of concern about Tony. "You can go to a hotel for a while, until the boat is released. We can help you find a place."

Before Angie could add to her statements, Deirdre placed both of her hands against her head and started to tremble. "I don't have access to any money. Tony was going to set up a checking account at the bank in town, but he hadn't done it yet."

Jenna spoke in a comforting tone. "Do you have a credit card? Just use that."

"No." Deirdre set her jaw and looked out the window. "I don't have a credit card. We only have one." Her eyes flashed. "It's in Tony's name. It's in his wallet."

Jenna and Angie made eye contact.

Jenna leaned forward. "Our sister, Ellie, runs a bed and breakfast inn here in Sweet Cove. I know there was a cancellation for the coming week. I'll give Ellie a call and see if the room is still available." She carried her phone and went outside to make the call.

Deirdre stared after Jenna seemingly unable to comprehend, and then she turned to Angie. "I can't pay for the room."

"Don't worry about that right now. Do you have family nearby? A friend you could call?" Angie asked.

Something flickered over Deirdre's face. "I only have Tony and Brendan. There isn't anyone to call." She wrung her hands together.

Angie's heart squeezed for the woman's plight. She couldn't imagine not having her sisters or Mr. Finch, her boyfriend, Josh or Chief Martin to call if she needed help. How awful to be completely on your own without a friend or family member or a home to return to. She had to clear her throat. "It will be okay." She knew the words must sound empty and hollow.

Jenna came back in from outside the studio. "Ellie says the room has been reserved, but that she can do some juggling and put those people up in one of the carriage house apartments. They're repeat customers and have stayed in the carriage house before and they loved it."

"There, it's all set." Angie forced a smile. "You can stay at the B and B for the week while you look for something more permanent or your boat becomes available."

"Thank you." Deirdre breathed such a heavy sigh that her skinny shoulders shook.

Brendan pulled himself up in the crib and started to fuss.

Angie looked at the rosy-cheeked little boy and a zing of sadness squeezed her heart. She couldn't deny that there was plenty to be fussing about.

CHAPTER 6

Angie and Jenna helped the young woman pack up her few belongings, close up the port-a-crib, and put a few of the groceries in a canvas bag. Jenna had called Courtney to see if she could get away from the candy store to come pick them up. The youngest Roseland sister was always ready to tackle a mystery so she arranged with an employee to watch the store until evening. Courtney borrowed Ellie's van and picked up Mr. Finch who also wouldn't pass up a chance to do some investigating. They left the cats at home.

Parking in front of the studio apartment, Courtney stepped out of the van. "What's cookin'?"

"Plenty," Angie said softly as she carried the folded up crib to the rear of the vehicle. "Despite this woman's predicament, I'm wondering if we're inviting a murderer into our home."

Courtney glanced at the young mom who was tending to her son. "Well, you know how the saying goes … keep enemies closer. Having her nearby will give us a good chance to get information out of her." She opened the hatch and lifted the crib into the back of the van. "Remain skeptical, Sis. Don't let that soft heart of yours work against any clues that come up and point to her."

Mr. Finch got out and introduced himself to Deirdre and turned to Brendan. "What a fine young man." Brendan looked at Finch's cane with wide eyes and reached out to put his small fingers on the shiny wood.

"This is my cane. It helps me walk," Finch explained.

The little boy smiled at the older man.

Angie suggested to Deirdre that she give the landlady her cell phone number, but Deirdre said that she couldn't find her phone and must have left it on the boat. Angie wrote her own cell number and the address of the B and B on a piece of paper and, after giving it to the landlady in case Tony returned to the studio, she texted Chief Martin with news of Mrs. Collins's move to the Roseland's inn.

After loading the van and driving the short distance to the center of Sweet Cove, Courtney pulled into the Victorian's driveway and parked.

"Here we are," Mr. Finch announced. "Home sweet home."

"It's lovely." Deirdre admired the beautiful house with its sweeping wrap-around porch.

Ellie stood on the porch at the front door with keys in her hand. Euclid and Circe sat beside her. She greeted the woman and her little boy. "I had second thoughts about the arrangements. I thought it would be better if you had more privacy and putting you in one of the carriage house apartments would be better for a small child. You won't feel that he's disturbing the other guests if he's crying and the place has two small bedrooms and a full kitchen. It might suit your needs better." She gestured for Deirdre to follow her to the end of the driveway to the carriage house.

"I lived in the apartment for a short time." Mr. Finch smiled. "I found it most comfortable."

They helped carry the small suitcases and the crib up the stairs. Deirdre cried tears of gratitude when she saw the place. Ellie discreetly handed the woman an envelope of cash. "Here's some money to get you through the week, for groceries or whatever you need. I put some things in the fridge for you. And let us know if you ever need us to watch Brendan for a little while." When things were settled, the girls, the cats, and Mr. Finch returned to the house to make dinner.

Courtney removed hamburgers and veggie burgers from the fridge. "Let's just make a quick, simple dinner tonight."

Ellie said, "I walked to the farmer's market on the town common and bought some ears of corn and vegetables for a green salad."

"There are strawberries and goat cheese, too." Jenna carried the items to the center island counter. "Let's put them in the salad."

Mr. Finch leaned against the counter and started to shuck the corn over the trash can. As everyone worked at a task, Angie and Jenna told the others what they'd learned from Louisa at the Coveside coffee shop and from Deirdre when they showed up at the apartment.

"Do you think it's weird that she doesn't talk about her husband much?" Courtney pulled out a broiler pan. "Is it because she's in shock over what happened or is she afraid to say much in case she slips and makes a comment implicating her in killing Tony?"

"We aren't sure he's dead." Ellie reminded them. "He might still be alive."

"Well, if he isn't dead, then where is he?" Jenna washed the strawberries in the sink.

"What do you think about the amnesia idea?" Angie asked.

Mr. Finch replied. "I believe that such a thing is quite rare. I might be quick to dismiss that notion, but I suppose it is a possibility."

"What if he just took off?" Courtney set the broiler to high and placed the burgers on the pan. "What if he planned for months to fake his death to run away from the family?"

Angie looked at her youngest sister with wide eyes. "Wow. I didn't think of that."

"Maybe he's been squirreling money away for a long time." Jenna sliced the berries. "Deirdre doesn't have access to their accounts and no money of her own. Tony could be controlling the funds and keeping Deirdre in the dark so he can siphon money to his own private account."

"Don't you find it odd that Deirdre is so dependent on Tony?" Angie decided to bake some brownies to serve for dessert. She added ingredients to a big glass bowl. "She doesn't have her own credit card. She doesn't have access to any cash or to a bank account."

"Tony seems to be a very controlling person." Courtney scowled.

"What about what the waitress told you about Tony flirting with her?" Finch finished removing the husks from the corn on the cob and he placed them one by one into a pot of boiling water. "I wonder if he has a history of cheating on his wife. It might be something to investigate."

Jenna tilted her head in thought. "That could be telling. Maybe Deirdre had enough of Tony controlling her and the finances. Maybe he was a cheat and she'd had enough of that, too."

The cats listened intently to the conversation from on top of the fridge. Euclid hissed.

"If those things are true," Courtney said, "that gives Deirdre motive. And she certainly had opportunity being alone with Tony on the boat. She could have waited until the little boy was asleep and then went up to the deck where she crept up behind her husband." Courtney tiptoed across the room and snuck up behind Angie who was concentrating on blending the brownie mixture together.

Courtney said dramatically, "And then she pushed him over the side of the boat." She lunged and grabbed Angie around the waist pretending to knock her over.

Angie let out a shriek of surprise and tried to bat her sister with the wooden spoon. Everyone chuckled and Courtney scurried away from her sister's reach.

"I was just demonstrating how easy it would be to sneak up on someone and push them over." Courtney's eyes sparkled with mischief. "I thought the example was important to our investigation."

Angie shot her a look. "No brownies for you."

"We need to talk to Deirdre." Courtney peeked into the oven to check on the burgers. "Get her to talk about the night on the boat. Talk about where they went and what they did when they visited the island."

"I think we should go back to Coveside and talk to people on the docks," Jenna said. "Find out more about Tony."

"Does the man have any relatives besides his wife and son?" Finch went to the counter and pulled himself up onto a stool. "What about friends, former colleagues, boating associates?"

"Good idea." Angie poured the brownie mixture into a pan. "I'll ask the chief if he knows anyone we can talk to who knew Tony." She glanced at the back door. "I'd love to pick Deirdre's brain, but I think we should give her the night off before we start interrogating her."

"The poor woman's been through enough for one day." Ellie put some condiments on a tray.

"Would you say that if you knew she was guilty?" Jenna finished tossing the salad.

"Not every guilty person is a monster." Mr. Finch reached for his cane.

The two cats trilled causing everyone to look up at them.

Ellie said, "Well, it seems that the cats approve of your statement Mr. Finch."

Courtney cocked her head at Euclid. "You agree with Mr. Finch? Huh. I didn't expect that of you. I thought you only saw things in black and white."

"I believe Euclid has a unique way of viewing the world." Mr. Finch looked over the top of his glasses at the cat. "Indeed, he has a strong sense of right and wrong. But he also has a compassionate, loving heart. Crimes are always wrong and we can hate what happened, but that doesn't mean we have to hate the criminal."

"You're right." Ellie nodded at Finch. "Think back to the case of the bomb in your house. The two men involved in that mess had both suffered from abusive fathers. That's certainly not an excuse for one of them to have turned bad, but there are sometimes sad circumstances that lead people to a criminal path."

The girls picked up the platters of food and

headed into the hall. The huge orange cat flicked his plume of a tail and jumped down off the fridge to follow the family into the dining room. Circe licked a paw, leaped to the floor, and joined the line leaving the kitchen.

As they entered the hall, Mr. Finch leaned closer to Angie and winked. "I also believe that a certain sweet black feline has softened the nature of our fine orange boy."

Angie smiled as she watched the two cats walking side by side into the dining room.

CHAPTER 7

Courtney started out the front door of the Victorian to head to the candy store for the evening shift. She looked back at Mr. Finch sitting at the dining table arranging the cards. "Tell Rufus not to forget to come to the store to walk me home. He gets so engrossed in the game that he might not remember to come get me." She winked at Finch. "And try not to beat him too badly."

It was game night at the Victorian and the group had set out different board games, cards, and puzzles. More often than not, Finch, Courtney, Tom, and Courtney's boyfriend, Rufus engaged in a heated competition with cards, Ellie, Jack Ford, and Josh Williams played Scrabble, and Jenna and Angie did a puzzle at the end of the dining table. Any of the B and B guests who were at the inn were always welcome to join in. The girls had put out snacks and sweets on the buffet table including mascarpone dip with cannoli cookies, red velvet cupcakes, and chocolate chip bars.

Rufus Fudge rang the bell and entered the foyer

carrying a bag of tortilla chips and a container of salsa. Jack Ford came in right behind Rufus with a bottle of wine. Jack wore a bow tie and a forest green cardigan. His evening neckwear was bright green and had tiny gold Scrabble squares printed on the fabric.

Ellie hugged Jack and took his hand. "What a perfect tie. I love it."

Jack was often reserved and formal, but when he was around Ellie he practically glowed. "I found it on the internet."

Rufus sat down across from Finch. "I told Jack it doesn't matter what design is on his bow tie, it still makes him look like a nerd." Rufus was interning for the summer in Ford's law office.

"If you were a real employee, I'd fire you," Jack replied with a deadpan expression. The two got along well, but they both enjoyed the verbal sparring.

Tom and Josh arrived at the same time and each was greeted with a hug and a kiss from their girlfriends.

"I didn't have time to stop for anything." Josh wrapped his arm around Angie and they walked to the table.

She beamed at him. "You don't need to bring anything. You know we always have plenty of food and drink here."

The last person to enter was Betty Hayes, Finch's lady friend. She bustled through the door out of

J.A Whiting

breath and with flushed cheeks. "I was afraid I was late." She rushed over to Mr. Finch and hugged him nearly burying his face in her ample chest. When she stepped back, Finch's eyeglasses were askew on his face and some strands of his hair were sticking straight up. Betty smoothed down the unruly locks.

Betty was taking Courtney's place at the card-playing end of the table and she sat down next to Finch. "I haven't played cards for ages. Don't let that make you think you'll beat me." She batted her eyelashes at Mr. Finch. "I'm quite good, you know. And very competitive."

"I am not a bit surprised," Finch admitted. "I would expect nothing less."

The games began and conversation eventually turned to the missing Tony Collins.

Ellie said, "We happen to have Mrs. Collins staying here at the B and B with her little boy."

Surprised faces turned to her.

"They're in one of the carriage house apartments."

The sisters explained how they'd been at Chief Martin's aunt's house and saw the grounded boat, helped the young woman and her child from the vessel, and ended up inviting them to stay with them when she had to leave the studio apartment. A discussion started about what could have happened to Mr. Collins and whether or not Deirdre could have killed her husband.

60

"Deirdre acted odd when she came off the boat." Jenna explained the woman's behavior and how she hadn't considered notifying the police that her husband was not on the boat.

Jack narrowed his eyes. "Had they been drinking?"

"She claimed to have had a migraine coming on," Angie said. "Which is why she slept so soundly and for such a long time."

"That was convenient, wasn't it?" Jack looked suspicious. "She is sound asleep when her husband goes missing."

The girls told them about Tony's controlling ways and his flirtatious actions with the waitress at the Coveside coffee shop.

Betty grumped. "This man sounds like a real bad apple. I'd have kicked him to the curb long ago."

Angie believed the statement. Betty was an independent woman who would not take guff from any man.

Betty added, "Maybe he got what he deserved."

"Miss Betty," Finch chided his sweetheart.

Betty touched the side of the older man's face. "I'm not as kind or forgiving as you are, Victor." She sighed. "Let's talk about something more pleasant." She looked over at Jenna and Tom. "I can show you the house at the end of the week if that works for you. The owner has agreed to let you in again."

Tom had made an offer on an old house two doors down from the Victorian. It had suffered years of neglect and needed a lot of work. Tom wanted Jenna to see it before completing the purchase since it would belong to both of them once they were married.

"I can't wait to see the house." Jenna beamed.

"Just remember it's in a state of disrepair. It's going to take time to restore it to its original glory." Tom eyed his sweetie.

"You can do anything." Jenna smiled. "When you're done with it, it will be gorgeous."

Angie's phone buzzed. "It's Chief Martin. I'll take it in the kitchen." She got up and left the room.

Ellie and Jenna exchanged looks.

"Why is the chief calling Angie?" Josh asked.

Ellie piped up. "Sometimes he asks for our help with things."

Josh, Jack, Rufus, and Betty had no idea that the sisters and Mr. Finch had some paranormal skills. Tom had recently been told about what the girls were capable of and he'd taken it well, which was a huge relief to Jenna.

Josh was about to ask another question when Tom spoke trying to cover for the sisters. "Remember the girls have had grief counseling training? You recall the chief called on them when the murder happened at the resort."

Josh gave a slight nod, but it was obvious that he

still seemed unclear about how the sisters might be of assistance to the chief.

Looking at the cards in his hand, Rufus said, "Maybe the sisters all have magical powers and they use their skills to help the chief solve the crime."

Ellie's eyes nearly fell from her head and her jaw dropped.

Jenna cleared her throat and deflected Rufus's comment by teasing, "You never know, do you?"

Angie returned and took her seat. Her lips turned down and her eyes had lost their sparkle. "The chief says a body was found on the rocks in Silver Cove. It's a man about the same age as Tony Collins. A positive ID will be done soon."

Everyone was silent for a few moments, and then Jenna asked, "He hasn't spoken with Deirdre?"

Angie shook her head. "Chief Martin will make a visit if it turns out to be her husband."

"Well, it must be him." Betty set her jaw. "Dead people don't wash up on our shores every day."

"Did he call just to let us know?" Jenna eyed her sister.

Angie looked up. "He'd like us to meet him at the coroner's office."

"Now?" Ellie's eyes were wide.

"In about an hour."

"That puts a damper on game night." Betty put her cards on the table.

"All of you stay and have fun." Angie forced a bright tone to her voice.

"Why does the chief need you at the coroner's office?" Josh looked confused.

Ellie responded, "When next of kin arrive, it's very helpful to have a counselor present."

"But you aren't working as counselors despite your training." Josh straightened. "Why don't the police have a professional counselor on staff? Or on standby? Someone with lots of experience?"

Jenna swallowed. "The police department has to work within a very small budget. There are people on consult, but sometimes they aren't available, so we get called."

Ellie folded her hands. "And we do a very good job."

Angie hated having to dance around the truth. She felt like crying. She wanted to tell Josh, but was afraid to lose him when he heard about their skills. "I'm going to get a cup of tea." She put a smile on her face. "Would anyone like something?" The others answered in the negative and she stood up and headed to the kitchen.

When she was pouring the hot water into a mug, Josh came into the kitchen and put his arm around Angie's shoulders. "Are you okay?"

She gave him a little smile and nodded. "There's just been a lot going on in town recently. It can be ... well, difficult."

Josh wrapped her in his arms. "You can decline the chief's request, you know."

Angie let out a sigh. "I would hate to do that."

She looked up at Josh and his warm eyes melted her heart. She decided to stop hiding things from him. "There's something I want to tell you about."

Just as she was about to go on, Betty bustled into the kitchen. "Victor would like a hot toddy and I offered to make one for him." She opened one of the cabinets. "Oh, your phone rang again, Angie. It's Chief Martin. Jenna is talking to him."

A worried look spread over the young woman's face. She took Josh's hand and led him to the hall. "Let's go see what he wants."

They entered the dining room as Jenna clicked off from the call. "Chief Martin says the body is not that of Tony Collins. There was a wallet with identification in the man's pocket. His name is Patrick Ackerman. The chief is researching who he is and where he came from."

"Well." Angie's forehead scrunched. "A dead body that isn't Tony Collins? What's going on?"

"We'll find out tomorrow," Jenna said. "All of that can wait. For now, let's enjoy our evening together. We can worry about other things in the morning." She made eye contact with Angie.

Angie nodded and squeezed Josh's hand. "Jenna's right." She kissed his cheek and pulled him to the table. She wouldn't let trouble interfere with their time together.

Josh whispered, "You wanted to tell me about something?"

Angie smiled. "That can wait, too. Right now,

I'm going to beat you at Scrabble."

Rufus tsked and shook his head. "Such a competitive bunch of people."

"And you're one of them," Ellie told him with a smile.

Everyone chuckled and returned to their games.

Trouble would still be there in the morning. It wasn't going anywhere.

CHAPTER 8

"You told me that you and your husband went to Marion Island so that he could meet with a business associate. Was Patrick Ackerman the person he was meeting?"

Deirdre sat at the small kitchen table in the carriage house apartment. Angie and Jenna sat at the table with Deirdre and Chief Martin while Courtney played with Brendan on the floor building towers with blocks.

Deirdre wrung her hands. "I don't know who he met with. Tony never talked business with me. Like I told you, I took Brendan to the beach that day. After that, we wandered around the town, got ice cream, had some dinner. Tony was busy all day. We didn't see him at all until it was time to go home. I took Brendan back to the boat and we played on the deck and then went inside to rest until Tony came back."

"When Tony returned to the boat did he have any guests with him?"

"I told you before. I was below with Brendan. I

67

didn't go up on deck." Deirdre's eyebrows pinched together for a few moments. "I woke up when Tony came down to check on us. He said we'd leave the island in about an hour. Maybe I heard voices on deck. I just didn't pay any attention. I never did. Sometimes Tony had an associate visit and they'd have a drink together on deck. I never paid attention to who he was with. I didn't care. Brendan was sleeping soundly that night and I was comfortable, so I fell back to sleep."

The chief placed a photo of Ackerman on the table. "Do you recognize this man?"

Deirdre took a quick look. She shook her head.

"Would you take another look?" The chief put his finger on the photo and slid it closer to the woman. "Have you ever seen this man before?"

"I don't recognize him. Is this Patrick Ackerman?" Deirdre's fingers trembled. "Did he do something to Tony?"

"Mr. Ackerman's body washed ashore in Silver Cove last evening." The chief's face was solemn.

Deirdre sucked in a breath, her eyes wide in horror.

"Mr. Ackerman had business dealings with your husband. He was on Marion Island the same day you and your husband were there."

"I never met him." The young woman's eyes looked sunken in her pale face.

A flicker of disbelief zinged through Angie's body. She wasn't sure if the source of the warning was Deirdre's denial of meeting Ackerman or something else about the case.

"Have you found Tony yet?" Deirdre eyed the chief from under her long brown lashes. Angie thought she appeared more shrunken and low energy than ever.

"The search is still underway." The chief rose from his seat. "Thank you for your time, Mrs. Collins. You should be able to return to your boat in about three or four days." Deirdre didn't seem happy about that news.

The three girls and the chief exited the apartment and walked to the garden pergola behind the Victorian to sit on the patio in the Adirondack chairs.

"Any sensations from the woman?"

"I don't think Deirdre is being forthcoming." Jenna rested back in the chair.

"I agree," Angie said. "I get the feeling she isn't telling all she knows."

Courtney chimed in. "I wasn't watching her since I was playing with Brendan, but her voice carries tones of untruth. I can't explain it. It just doesn't feel right."

"You mean it doesn't *sound* right," Jenna corrected.

Courtney tilted her head to the side. "No. It doesn't *feel* right when she's speaking. Her words make my skin feel funny. Her words have negative energy and pick at my skin. I think she's lying. At least about some things."

"I get that very same feeling over my skin sometimes." Angie rubbed her arms thinking about the sensation.

"It might be time for one of Angie's truth muffins." Courtney grinned.

"Bah," Angie growled.

"What's this?" The chief looked intrigued.

Jenna explained that when they first met Mr. Finch they suspected him of murdering his brother and that Angie seems to have the ability to put intention into what she bakes. Courtney suggested that Angie bake a "truth" muffin and feed it to Mr. Finch to find out if he would confess to the crime or not. The experiment backfired and for a few hours, Finch fell in love with Angie.

"It was a complete failure." Angie rolled her eyes.

Courtney said, "I keep telling you, Sis, you just need to practice."

"The only thing I seem to be able to do is put good feelings into what I bake and people's moods get happier when they eat the treats."

"Have you baked anything recently that contains good feelings?" The chief looked at Angie. "I could use one of those right about now."

"You mentioned that Tony Collins and Ackerman were business partners?" Jenna asked.

The chief said, "It seems they were planning a joint venture. It was still in the initial stages.

Sources report that Ackerman was on Marion Island the day the Collins family visited." The chief raised an eyebrow. "Are you girls interested in a trip to the island? It might be helpful to walk around. Talk to people. See if you can pick up on anything."

"I'm off today," Courtney said. "I wouldn't mind visiting the island. Let's go."

Angie blinked. "I don't know. I have some things to do to get the bake shop ready."

"Do them tomorrow." Courtney stood up. "It's still early in the day. We can get there before lunch. It would be nice to spend time with my sisters." Courtney winked. "And do some sleuthing."

"My jewelry production is going well," Jenna said. "I can go today."

"Come on." Courtney pulled Angie from the chair. "You need an outing."

Angie scowled. "I need an outing, but one that doesn't involve death and criminals."

Courtney stood before her older sister. "There are still good people in the world, Sis. Focus on that. Focus on using your powers to bring justice to the world." Courtney smiled. "It's sort of like being super heroes."

Angie couldn't keep a smile from forming. "I'll keep that in mind." She turned for the back door of the house. "Let's get our things."

CHAPTER 9

The three sisters stepped down the gangplank after an hour and a half ferry ride to Marion Island. Ellie remained at home as expected. The town was similar to Sweet Cove with old-fashioned streetlamps, flowers everywhere, and brick sidewalks lined with stores, cafes, and restaurants. There were places to rent bikes to ride around the island on the extensive bicycle paths that led to the harbor, white-sand beaches, and quaint little outlying towns. Although it would have been fun to visit some of the other towns, the girls only needed to walk around Main Town for their sleuthing since Tony and Deirdre had spent their day there.

"I wish we brought our swimsuits. It's a gorgeous day." Courtney loved to body surf and several of the island's beaches had large, powerful waves.

"This is a working trip, remember?" Jenna teased.

"Can we at least stop for lunch?" Courtney eyed a pretty café with outside seating. "I'm starving."

"Let's eat then," Angie agreed. "We need to fortify ourselves for our afternoon of investigating."

The girls were seated at a table with an umbrella where they had a great view of the harbor and the tourists walking around the town. Looking over the menu, the three sisters sipped cold drinks.

"Where should we start our investigation?" Courtney eyed the shops.

"I guess we could start right here." Jenna took the pictures from her purse that Police Chief Martin had given her of Collins and Ackerman. "We can ask the staff at some of these restaurants and stores if they recognize either of the men."

"Then we should go down to the harbor and ask around there." Angie sipped from her straw. "Maybe we could talk to the harbor master and find out where Tony moored his boat that day."

The waitress returned and took their lunch orders, but before she turned away, Jenna pointed to the pictures on the table. "We were wondering if you could help us. Do you recognize either of these men?"

The young waitress had her sandy colored hair in a loose bun. She eyed the sisters with suspicion.

"We're consultants working on a crime," Courtney told the waitress. "This man's body washed up in Silver Cove last night. We know he spent time here on the island right before he died."

"We're just gathering information," Angie told the waitress. "Then we pass it on to the police analysts for them to review." She thought the young woman might be more forthcoming if she was assured that they were not police officers. Angie smiled encouragingly.

The waitress peered at the pictures and her face hardened. She placed her finger on Tony's picture. "This one was here the other day." She tapped the photo hard several times. "Hope you aren't friends with him, 'cuz he's a real jerk."

"Why?" Angie asked. "Was he rude to you?"

"He was with a woman. Pretty. He seemed like Mr. Big Shot. When the girl got up to go to the bathroom, the jerk pinched my butt when I dropped the check off at the table." She shook her head in disgust. "I gave him a dirty look and walked away. I would have liked to pour a drink over his head."

"Too bad you didn't." Jenna scowled at Tony's antics. "Did anyone else join them? Was anyone else with them?"

"Nope, just the girl and the jerk."

"And a little boy?" Courtney asked.

"There wasn't any kid with them." The waitress shook her head. "It was just the two of them flirting with each other."

Angie sat up. "What did the woman look like?"

"She was cute, slender. She had long black hair. The ends were dyed blue." The waitress looked across the patio. "I need to see to the other tables."

The sisters stared at each other.

"Louisa," Jenna said. "It must have been her."

Courtney looked surprised. "Louisa, from the Coveside coffee shop? Wow. Why did she bother with a guy like Tony? A married guy."

Angie clarified. "Louisa told us she didn't know Tony was married until the news spread that he was missing. Tony must have conveniently kept that to himself."

"He was good looking," Jenna noted. "He seemed loaded with money, had a nice boat. He probably flashed money around."

"I'm sure he gave Louisa lots of attention. She probably felt flattered." Angie made a face thinking about the lying, cheating Tony.

Courtney leaned forward and whispered. "Maybe Louisa and Tony ran into Deirdre and the baby." She paused for effect. "Maybe Louisa was infuriated that Tony was married, that he lied to her." She raised her eyebrows.

"You think Louisa had something to do with Tony's disappearance?" Jenna put her chin in her hand and narrowed her eyes.

"She might have blown her top and decided to get revenge. Maybe she hid on the boat and pushed him over when they were underway," Courtney speculated.

"Then how did she get off the boat?" Angie tried to think of a way Louisa could push Tony overboard and then somehow get away.

Courtney offered a guess. "She could have

75

stayed on the boat and deliberately grounded it."

"Huh." Jenna thought it over. "That would sure be taking a chance. What if Deirdre went up to the deck?"

Courtney had an idea. "Then maybe Louisa would have tossed Deirdre over the side, too."

"Yikes." Angie's face clouded. "But I guess people have killed over less."

"Indeed." Courtney frowned.

"Here's a thought," Jenna said. "Is the person who killed Ackerman responsible for Tony's disappearance?"

"I was wondering that very same thing." Angie looked across the street to the harbor. "Did someone have it in for both of them?"

"Or did someone want one of them dead and the other one got in the way and ended up getting killed, too?" Courtney leaned back and crossed her arms.

"What a mess." Angie lifted her glass. "We have a lot of work to do."

***

AFTER LUNCH, the sisters wandered around the stores showing the two men's pictures to employees. One of the people manning the ice cream stand recalled waiting on Tony and the young woman with black hair. He didn't see where they headed with their ice cream cones. It was a busy day and he didn't pay attention to them after they strolled away.

"Let's hit the harbor." Angie led the way down the street to the walkway that ran along the water. The boats bobbing in the gentle current made a picturesque scene. "There's the harbor master's office. I'll go ask where Tony docked that day."

Jenna and Courtney continued walking to the wharves to show the pictures to boat owners. No one they talked to recognized either of the men. After talking with the harbor master, Angie caught up with her sisters and pointed out the spot where Tony had been assigned to dock. "The man said there are boats still down there that were docked near Tony that day."

The sisters stopped to talk to a man who looked to be in his sixties. They showed him the pictures.

"This guy." He pointed to Tony's photograph. "Yup, he was here. People come and go, but I remember this guy. He came close when he was bringing his boat in. Too close. I gave him a look of concern and he shot me a comment. He said something like, 'Don't worry, old man. I know what I'm doing.'" He seemed real arrogant. I ignored him after that."

"Was he with other people?" Jenna asked.

"There was a woman and child on the boat. I assumed it was his wife. Could have been a friend or a sister, I suppose. I didn't see them together much. The woman came back late with the little

77

boy and went below. I was sitting back here." He gestured to the outside seating area on his boat. "I had a glass of wine. It was a nice night." He nodded to the picture. "That guy came back with another man. They sat outside on the boat. I went below then, didn't see anything else. The boat's engines started up when I was in bed. They left the dock. I wasn't sorry to hear them go."

"Did you see a pretty woman with long black hair around the boat?"

The man's forehead wrinkled, and then he shook his head. "I didn't see anyone like that. The woman with the child didn't have long hair and it wasn't black."

The girls thanked him for his help and wandered away.

"So what do we know?" Courtney asked. "Tony Collins is missing. He was here to meet with a business associate who we can assume was Patrick Ackerman."

Jenna added, "Deirdre and Brendan were on the boat. They spent the day apart from Tony and returned to the boat in the evening."

"Tony had lunch with a woman." Angie pulled her hair into a ponytail to keep it from blowing in her face. "It might have been Louisa."

Courtney said, "You mean it *probably* was Louisa."

Angie continued. "It's possible that a man sat on the boat with Tony before heading back to Sweet

78

Cove. Deirdre wasn't sure about that, but this man we just talked to claims Tony had a male visitor. Maybe it was Ackerman."

Jenna said, "Ackerman washed up dead in Silver Cove."

"So here's a thought." Courtney looked out over the harbor. "Tony kills Ackerman and takes off. He's still alive and running from the murder he committed."

Angie stopped. "That could be the answer to this."

"Well, how did he kill Ackerman?" Jenna wasn't convinced. "While they were sitting on the boat in the harbor? They're docked there and Tony just tosses the body overboard?"

Angie bit her lip. "Tony could have killed Ackerman on the way back to Sweet Cove."

"Wouldn't Deirdre have known if another guy was on the boat all that time?" Jenna asked.

"What about Louisa?" Courtney reminded her sisters that Louisa might have gone nuts when she learned that Tony had a wife and child. "Louisa could have hidden on the boat and attacked Tony on the return trip."

Jenna frowned. "Again, wouldn't Deirdre have heard a fight? She claims not to have heard anything. She can't be that sound a sleeper."

Angie let out a sigh. "Let's go home. We can talk it over with Ellie and Chief Martin and Mr. Finch."

Courtney put her hands through her sisters'

arms. "We better tell the cats, too."

The girls headed for the ferry for the evening trip back to Sweet Cove.

CHAPTER 10

Angie stood in her new café letting her eyes rove over the beautiful work done by Tom. Euclid and Circe sat next to her. The beadwork on the walls had been installed and white-washed, the granite and marble countertops were in place, the cabinetry was ready and waiting for dishes and glasses and mugs.

She let out a happy sigh and walked to the new door that led outside to the wraparound porch. A few café tables and chairs would be placed on the porch for the bake shop customers. The new window that Tom installed even had a window box and Angie had planted geraniums, impatiens, and greens in it so that the plants would get bigger and fill in the space prior to the grand opening. Angie had ordered a new sign to be fashioned from wood with a cupcake carved into the design and painted in gold, rose, and light pink.

Later in the day, she and Jenna and Tom were going to move some of the boxes containing dishes and baking pans from the storage room of the carriage house to the new bake shop so Angie could start getting things in order. A smile spread over her face. She couldn't wait to open.

A man's voice spoke behind her. "Hey, there."

Angie turned to see Josh Williams coming up the steps. He carried a potted plant. "I brought this for you to celebrate your new shop." Josh's smile warmed Angie's heart which started beating double-time at the sight of the handsome man. He wrapped his right arm around her and gave her a sweet kiss. "I thought if I waited to give it to you on opening day then my plant would get lost in all the hoopla." He chuckled. "I need to make sure I get credit for my thoughtfulness."

Angie hugged him. "You never have to worry about such things. You could bring me a blade of grass and I'd put a gold star right next to your name." She beamed at Josh. "Make that a gold heart." She took the plant from him. "I have a plant stand in the storage room that will work beautifully with this. I'll put it right here near the door to the shop." She placed the fern on the porch floor.

"I saw Tom. He told me he's going to help you move some things into the store later today. I'd like to help. I'll meet you back here later this afternoon?"

Angie thanked him. Josh was always busy running the Sweet Cove resort and it was hard for him to get time off so she appreciated that he wanted to help her.

"I haven't heard any news about the missing man," Josh noted. He glanced down the driveway towards the carriage house apartments. "The poor woman and her son. She must be in a terrible state."

Angie looked around to see if anyone was nearby. "You know, she doesn't seem as upset as one might expect. She rarely mentions her husband. It's subtle and hard to describe, but I find her reaction to the whole mess to be kind of strange."

"Do you suspect her?" Josh kept his voice down.

"I think I have to. She was on the boat when her husband disappeared. She claims that there wasn't anyone else with them except their son, Brendan."

Josh's face took on a serious expression and after a few moments he asked, "When you found the boat could it be possible that someone was hiding inside?"

Angie's eyes went wide. "I wondered about that." She looked off across the yard, thinking. "That's certainly a possibility. Chief Martin helped carry the little boy off the boat and then he went up the ladder to help Deirdre. None of us climbed aboard just then. Chief Martin returned to the boat later to see if Collins might be hurt somewhere on board." Angie looked at Josh. "Someone could have climbed out and snuck off when we all went up to the chief's aunt's house." Her hand touched

Josh's arm. "Tony Collins could have been hiding in the boat."

"Maybe that's why Mrs. Collins is acting so oddly," Josh said. "She could be covering for her husband."

Angie held Josh's hand and smiled at him. "You're a genius. Maybe you should change careers and become a detective."

***

ANGIE WALKED into Jenna's jewelry shop. "I think we should go up to Chief Martin's aunt's place." She explained the conversation she'd had with Josh about someone possibly hiding in the Collins's boat. Jenna put her crimping tool on the desk next to the mat holding an array of dark green and aqua stones.

"What would returning accomplish?" Jenna wondered what her sister had in mind.

"I want to look around. Go back down to the beach, check out the rocks and dunes, see if there are any paths that lead away from the sand. Look for any clues that someone might have snuck away over the rocks."

"It can't hurt. We should talk to the chief's aunt again anyway. We went there to try to figure out the things she was worried about." Jenna picked up the jar of sea glass that sat on the windowsill next to her and held it up to the light. The girls' nana had given Jenna the jar filled with colorful pieces of sea glass. "Sometimes I wonder if I'll ever see Nana again." About a month ago, Jenna saw the ghost of Nana in her shop. The spirit only stayed for less than a minute, but the sight of her grandmother filled Jenna with a warm, wonderful feeling of love.

"What makes you think of her?" Angie sat down in the chair next to the desk.

"I guess because of Tony Collins going missing and Deirdre being left behind. And Patrick Ackerman's body washing up. The sense of loss tugs at my heart. It makes me think of Mom and Dad and Nana."

Angie reached out and touched her sister's arm. "We can't just think of what we've lost. We still have so much." Angie was about to list all of their blessings when Jenna interrupted.

"Oh, I know that. I was thinking of Deirdre's loss and how she seems so alone and lonely and adrift, with no one and no home to turn to. We've always had each other. We've always loved and cared for each other. I love the Victorian and that we all live together. I feel bad for Deirdre and her predicament. It's so sad."

Angie's eyes welled up and she bit her lip. "We're very lucky to have one another." She nodded and gave Jenna's hand a squeeze.

Jenna smiled. "Come on, let's go do some investigating."

***

AFTER MAKING a call to Chief Martin and asking if Aunt Anna would mind if they came up to check out the spot where the boat was grounded, and getting the okay, Jenna and Angie drove to the outskirts of Sweet Cove with the two cats perched on the back seat. The girls thought it might be helpful having the cats along and Anna seemed to enjoy the felines the last time they visited. Jenna pulled the car into Anna's driveway. The older woman opened the front door, stepped onto the porch, and waved.

"How nice to see you." Anna's face lit up when she saw the cats emerge from the backseat. "Oh, you brought Euclid and Circe!" She bent to scratch their cheeks and the cats purred. "Wonderful creatures." She gave the girls a bright smile. "Phillip called to tell me that you'd like to take another look at where the boat was grounded. Would you like to have a look now? Then we can have some tea or a cold drink on the porch." She walked the girls to her backyard. "Is there something you hope to see? Something in particular you're looking for?"

Angie gave a shrug and a smile. "We don't know what we're looking for or what we hope to find."

Anna gave a hearty laugh. "Well, not to fret. An open mind can sometimes lead to discovery."

Anna's gardener was working on a cluster of

bushes near the back property line and he turned when he saw the three women approaching. He put his clippers on the ground, wiped his arm across his brow, and walked over. "Hey."

The girls greeted him. The cats stared at him noncommittally. "We were wondering if you ever noticed someone walking down on the beach?" Angie moved her hand in the direction of the path that led to the tiny bit of sand below the bluff.

Jacob made a face. "It really can't be called a beach. It's just some sand at the bottom of the cliff. You can walk from one side to the other in less than half a minute. It doesn't lead anywhere. It's hemmed in by the rocks on both sides. Nobody goes walking down there. They'd have to come through the yard to get to the sand." The man wiped his hands on his jeans. "This is private property. No one would come onto Mrs. Lincoln's back lawn to get down to the sand. No one would even know there was a path back here."

"Do boats ever land down there?" Jenna asked.

"Not to my knowledge, but I haven't been working here long."

"No." Anna shook her head. "It's only at low tide that there's any sand visible. No one ever lands their boat there."

Jenna and Anna headed for the path to the sand below the bluff.

Angie turned to the gardener and asked, "Have you ever seen anyone back here lurking around?"

Jacob gave her a surprised look. "No. What do you mean?"

"I just wondered if people might cut through Anna's backyard." Angie shifted her gaze to the grove of trees at the back. "What's on the other side of those trees?"

"I don't know. I don't do much work that far back. Right now, I'm just pulling out some of the pricker bushes." He pointed to where he was working. "Mrs. Lincoln thinks they're getting too big and encroaching on the yard. I never bothered to see what's on the other side of the trees."

Angie looked around. A good-sized red barn stood at the edge of the property. The cats had wandered over to it and were sniffing around. "What's in the barn?"

Jacob followed Angie's gaze. "Not much. Some lawn equipment, rakes, stuff like that."

Angie looked the gardener in the eyes. "You ever see or hear anything around here that seems out of place?"

The man cocked his head. "Like what?"

"I don't really know. I guess you'd know if you thought something was amiss." She scanned the yard one more time. Her eyes kept being drawn back to the barn.

Jenna called for Angie to come along. She and Aunt Anna were about to walk down the path.

Angie smiled at the gardener. "Thanks." She jogged over to the edge of the bluff and watched her sister and the older woman walk down to the bit of sand at the bottom. She stood still and closed her eyes for a few moments trying to tune into her senses. A buzzing of electricity pulsed in her blood. Her eyelids lifted. *There's something about this place.* Angie sighed, berating herself for not paying attention to her feelings when they were here previously. Her intuition told her that she was missing something important.

But what?

CHAPTER 11

"There are little slips of sandy spots up and down the coast," Anna told the girls. "Spots where there's a break in the rock formation with a bit of sand area. The places are usually very hard to access and as the tide comes in the sandy space disappears."

Angie and Jenna had walked around the tiny beach and saw that, besides the path from Anna's backyard, there were just rocky cliffs on both sides of the sand. The girls determined that it would be very hard to make a get-away from this spot unless a person used the path.

The cats sat at the top of the bluff watching the three women investigate the small beach.

"I wish we had thought to look for footprints when we were here the other day." Angie released a sigh of exasperation. "If someone had gone up the path before we got here, there would be footprints in the sand." While she was glancing around the rocks, she remembered something and her eyes lit up. "I'm going text Courtney. She took some pictures of the boat the day it got grounded." Angie hurriedly pulled her phone from her pocket and fired off a text to her sister. She, Jenna, and Anna paced around the area waiting for a reply from Courtney. After five minutes had passed, Angie received a text. As she read it, the corners of her mouth turned down. "Courtney looked at the photos on her phone. She says there's no indication of footprints near the boat or anywhere in the sand."

Aunt Anna and Jenna both let out a sigh.

Angie looked up and saw Euclid and Circe on the bluff watching her. She considered that if the cats were disinterested in what was on the beach then the area where the Collins's boat ran aground probably didn't hold any clues.

The women headed back up to Anna's yard and went to sit on the front porch of the farmhouse. Anna brought out cold drinks and a small bowl of water for the cats. They chatted for a few minutes and then, unsure if she should, Angie decided to bring up the subject that Chief Martin had shared with them. She made eye contact with Anna. "You know, Chief Martin, ah, Phillip told us about some odd things happening around your house."

Anna's eyes grew wide, but then her cheeks puffed as she blew out some air. "Phillip worries more than he should. I never should have told him my concerns."

"But those things had you worried." Jenna was of the mind that people should share things that bother them and she thought it was important to listen to intuition. "People often dismiss things when they shouldn't. When something seems off, it usually is."

Anna pursed her lips.

"Has anything worrisome happened recently?" Angie wondered if the episodes had come and gone, having some explanation like the wind blowing things around or maybe the gardener working in the yard when Anna didn't expect him.

Anna squeezed her hands together. "The last time was the night before you came to visit me."

The girls both leaned slightly forward at the same time. Angie asked, "Tell us what seemed wrong."

"I like to keep the windows open at night. I heard some noises coming from the backyard. I thought I saw a light flickering, but then I blinked and it was gone." Anna absentmindedly rubbed her hand over the smooth surface of the porch table. "I started to worry that I was losing it, imagining things. That thought bothered me more than thinking someone was in the backyard."

"What's beyond the tree line at the back of your property?" Something had been picking at Angie since they'd been in the yard.

"There's a spot of grass with some granite benches in a semi-circle. In the middle is a war memorial. The town plants flowers there and they lay a wreath on the monument on Veteran's Day.

It's a shady, pleasant spot to sit for a few minutes on the way to the center of town."

Angie perked up. "Is there a fence between the park and your property?"

"No." Anna shook her head. "Just the trees."

Angie stood up. "I'm going to go cut through and see what it looks like." She looked at Jenna.

"I'll come." Jenna followed Angie down the stairs and across the lawn to the tree line.

"We'll be right back," they told Anna.

Jacob was still clipping at the bushes and when he heard the girls approaching, he gave them a look of surprise. "What are you doing?"

Jenna pushed some branches aside and stepped over a bunch of vines as she entered the grove of trees. The cats bounded into the wooded area.

"We want to see the park over there." Angie followed after her sister.

"There isn't much to see," Jacob told them.

When they emerged on the other side, the little spot was just as Anna had described it. In the middle of a stone patio, there was a three-foot-tall slab of granite with a plague attached to it listing the names of people from Sweet Cove and Silver Cove who had died in wars. Four granite benches sat in a semi-circle around one side of the monument. A flag flew on a pole to the right and a ten-foot-wide section of grass ringed the patio. There was a small gravel parking spot off the road at the edge of the space on the other side of some bushes where town workers parked when they came to water flowers and mow the grass. Euclid and Circe had their noses to the ground sniffing around the spot.

Angie saw a sign indicating that this was a trolley stop. Trolleys ran from this end of Sweet Cove down to the Coveside section of town making stops along the way. The sisters stepped onto the sidewalk and gazed up and down the street. They were only two blocks from the village stores and art galleries that had clustered over the years in this outer edge of Sweet Cove. The street was lined with mostly residential homes, but two houses up, there was a gift store and a stained glass shop.

Euclid stared across the street and meowed, but the girls had turned away and didn't notice.

"Are you picking up on anything?" Jenna glanced all around.

"Something feels off, but I can't figure out what it is." Angie put a hand on her hip and turned in a circle. "Do you sense anything?"

Jenna looked at her sister with a serious expression. "I feel the same way you do. Maybe we should come back with Courtney and Mr. Finch."

The girls pushed their way through the trees and bushes back into Anna's yard. Jacob was working on the bushes at the far end of the tree line. As the two sisters passed the red barn on the way back to the porch, a tingle twitched over Angie's skin and she gave the structure her full attention. It looked sturdy and well-built and the walls appeared freshly painted. There were even boxes filled with flowers sitting just under each of the windows. The building was landscaped with a ring of tended green and white leafed euonymus bushes.

Circe and Euclid sat in front of the barn door staring at the sisters.

"Why are the cats sitting at the door?" A shudder ran down Jenna's spine and she looked at her sister.

Angie eyed Jenna. "Let's ask Anna if we can go in there."

Jenna let out a little moan, afraid of what they might discover.

Anna gave permission for the girls to enter the barn and she walked back with them and stood at the door of the building. "I just keep lawn equipment and a snow blower in here." She swung open the door and the girls entered a clean, neat, high-ceilinged storage area. Angie and Jenna each headed in a different direction walking slowly and looking around. They didn't really expect to find anything.

A shaft of light reached the floor of the barn from a window placed high in the eaves. Angie watched particles of dust shimmer and dance in the ray of sunlight and then she tilted her head to look up at the window. Wooden beams reached from side to side across the upper space. A hay loft stretched above her built halfway back from the front of the building. Angie kicked a dust bunny and started to walk to the side where the lawn equipment stood, but then something buzzed in her head and she stopped in her tracks. Her eyes flew back up to the hay loft where the two felines were looking down at her. "Jenna."

Her sister came up next to Angie. "What's up?"

"I think we should go up to the loft." Angie pointed.

Jenna looked and her heart sank when she saw the cats. "Okay. You go first." Her voice held a shiver of trepidation.

The two girls crossed to the wooden ladder that led to the loft. Angie placed her foot on the first rung and put her hands on the sides of the ladder. Up she went with Jenna following a few rungs behind.

At the top, Angie crawled off the ladder and stood up. Her eyes narrowed when she saw what was there. "Wait til you see this," she said to her sister.

"What is it?" Anna called to the girls. She didn't want to climb to the loft on the rickety ladder. "Is something wrong?" She squinted and tilted her head back.

Jenna reached the top and stood. "What's all this?"

Two mattresses lay on the floor of the loft with crisp white pillows, white sheets, and dark blue blankets neatly spread over the beds. A flashlight was placed on each mattress and there was a battery powered lantern on the floor. A large plastic bin was set to the side. Angie lifted the lid and peered inside.

Jenna bent to see. "Food?" There were boxes of crackers, two boxes of cereal, a container full of granola bars, bags of dried fruit, and a case of water bottles. "Is this some emergency space? Or is someone living up here?"

Angie pulled out her phone and took pictures of the setting so that she could show Anna what was in the loft. The girls walked around the rest of the loft area, but there wasn't anything else to see so they edged down the ladder to the barn floor. Angie showed the pictures to Anna. The older woman leaned her face close to the phone screen and let out a gasp. She glanced at the loft over her head. "What on earth?" She blinked at the sisters. "People are living in my barn?"

"It didn't look to me like anyone was using it yet." Angie looked to Jenna for confirmation.

"I agree. It's set up and ready, but the food and the beds seem untouched."

"I think we should tell Chief Martin. Phillip." Angie couldn't get used to calling the chief by his first name. "He should have a look."

"Do you lock the barn?" Jenna asked Anna.

The woman shook her head. "Never. I never saw a need." She flicked her eyes to the loft again. "Until now." Color rose in her cheeks and her lips turned down as her face took on an angry expression. "How dare someone think they can live in my barn, encroach on my home."

"I guess this explains the noises and the lights you've seen," Angie noted.

"Well," Anna forced a smile. "One good thing is that this proves I wasn't imagining things." She reached out and squeezed the girls' hands. "I never would have found this without you." She cocked her head. "What made you think to go up to the hay loft?"

"Oh." Angie shrugged a shoulder. "I don't really know," she fibbed, looking at the two cats.

Jenna piped up. "Angie's intuition is strong. Sometimes I think she's psychic." She pretended to be kidding. Angie gave her sister a horrified look.

Anna led the girls and the felines out of the barn and back to the house. "I'm going to get a sturdy lock to put on the barn door. Today."

Jacob came around from the back of his van. When he spotted the three women on the porch, he asked, "Everything okay?"

Anna smiled. "Just fine."

When Jacob disappeared around the corner of the house, Anna said, "I'm not telling anyone about what you found."

"Why not?" Jenna asked.

"I don't want people to think that I don't know what's happening on my own property." Anna plopped into one of the porch chairs. "So many people think old folks are incompetent." She narrowed her eyes. "But they're wrong."

Circe jumped onto the woman's lap and gave her a lick on the hand. Euclid trilled at Anna from his place on the porch rail.

Angie smiled. "The cats agree with you."

As Anna grinned at Euclid and stroked Circe's velvet fur, her tension and anger seemed to melt away. "Perhaps I should get a cat of my own."

CHAPTER 12

Ellie stood on a stool in the new bake shop putting dishes and glasses away on the shelves. Tom, Rufus, and Josh carried the last table and four chairs into the café and Angie directed where to place the pieces. The men returned to the carriage house storage room for the final three boxes, carried them in and placed them on the floor for Angie to sort through them. Tom had to get to a new home construction job so he kissed Jenna goodbye. Rufus was heading to his apartment to do some more work for Attorney Ford and Josh had to return to the resort for an evening function. Angie thanked them all for their help. She hugged Tom and Rufus and walked Josh out to the porch where she kissed him and watched him walk to his car.

Angie went back inside the bake shop to continue with her tasks. Jenna had a rolling cart next to the new gleaming refrigerator and was removing cartons of milk, eggs, sticks of butter, and cream containers and placing the items in the fridge. Blenders and a microwave stood on the other side of the room on the granite workspace.

Mr. Finch sorted and placed silverware into the drawers while leaning against the new cabinets, his cane hooked over the marble countertop. Euclid and Circe sat on the counter supervising his work. "You aren't allowed to be in here once the bake shop opens, you know," he warned the cats.

Euclid scowled.

Finch had already put a nail in the wall and carefully placed Angie's framed inspection certificate on the hook. The certificate was the official blessing from the town of Sweet Cove allowing the shop to open.

"Wow, the place looks beautiful." Courtney strode into the room still wearing her candy store apron. She ran her hand over the smooth surface of the marble on her way to try out one of the new café chairs. Settled in the seat, she smiled at Angie. "I'll have a hazelnut latte, please."

Angie ignored the request. "What am I going to do without you working here at the bake shop with me?" Courtney had often worked for Angie at the old shop on Main Street before the lease was not renewed necessitating the move to a new location. Courtney's time was now filled running her candy store.

"You'll have to hire someone else." Courtney raised her eyebrows. "But, of course, the person will never be able to fill my shoes."

As Jenna passed her youngest sister, she

pinched her shoulder. "You ate more than you sold. Now, Angie will actually be able to make a profit."

Courtney reached out to give Jenna a playful smack, but the brunette was too quick and scooted away with a chuckle.

"I have two part-time people hired already for the noon to three shifts." Angie ran a wet cloth over the café table tops. "Tomorrow I'm doing the last round of interviews for the two remaining morning spots. Jenna is going to work here with me for the first week to make sure things go smoothly." She straightened and looked around. "I can't believe it's almost time to open."

A knock on the door from the porch made everyone's heads turn at once. Chief Martin opened the door and entered. "Wow." He glanced around. "This is great." He looked at Angie. "I'm looking forward to coming in every morning for my coffee." The chief had been a regular at Angie's bake shop before she had to close.

Angie nodded. "It will be great to get back to normal and have all of the regulars here each morning." She searched the chief's face. "Is there any news about Tony Collins?"

The chief pointed to one of the new chairs. "May I?" He sat and everyone gathered around. The cats listened from their perch on the counter. "The Coast Guard had some interesting information." He placed his meaty hands on the table. "They were able to access the GPS records of the Collins's boat. It seems they left Marion Island around midnight, headed on a course towards Sweet Cove harbor. The weather took a turn for the worse just as they got underway with heavy rain and higher than normal seas. About three-quarters of the way into the trip, the GPS showed the boat behaving erratically, changing course every few minutes."

"Like someone had left the helm?" Jenna asked.

The chief nodded. "Their boat had an autopilot, but at this point in the trip it seemed to have been switched off and the boat moved as if no one was in charge."

"What does it mean?" Angie looked perplexed.

The chief let out a sigh. He turned his hands up. "That's anyone's guess."

Courtney speculated. "Could the sea conditions have caused Tony to fall overboard?"

"It seems possible."

Mr. Finch brought a mug of hot coffee and a small pitcher of cream to the table. The chief looked up gratefully. He added the cream to the steaming liquid, wrapped his hands around the mug and lifted it to his lips. He took a deep breath and thanked Finch.

"So maybe there is no crime to pursue?" Mr. Finch raised an eyebrow.

"Except for the body of Patrick Ackerman," the chief reminded the group. "Ackerman was seen on the Collins's boat an hour before they left the island. He either fell off their boat or...."

"Or someone helped him off." Courtney finished the chief's sentence.

"I knocked at the carriage house, but no one answered." The chief took a long swallow of his coffee. "I wanted to speak with Mrs. Collins. Is she still a guest here?"

"She is," Ellie confirmed. "She took her son out for a walk in the stroller. Is Mrs. Collins allowed back on their boat yet?"

The chief shook his head. "It's still being held for investigation, as is the family vehicle."

Angie sat down across from the chief. "Did Aunt Anna call you about what we found in the barn?"

"She did indeed." Chief Martin looked weary.

Courtney's eyes grew wide. "What did you find in the barn?"

The girls told her about the beds and the container of food found in the hay loft and Courtney nearly jumped from her chair. "That's nuts. What's that about?" She gazed across the room looking at nothing, trying to make some sense of the news.

Angie turned to Courtney. "We thought that you and Mr. Finch should return with us to the barn. Have you look around. See what you think." She narrowed her eyes. "Or see what you sense."

Courtney nodded. "I'd be glad to. The barn thing is as weird as the way Deirdre behaved on the boat." She got up and headed into the main part of the house. "I need a shower. And a heavy dose of normal."

"I think you'll have a long wait for that." Ellie went to the cabinet to finish placing glassware on the shelves.

Angie's phone buzzed with an incoming call. "I don't recognize the number. I'll take it on the porch."

Everyone chatted about things unrelated to crime until Angie came back inside. She blinked. "That was the landlady who owns the studio apartment that the Collins had rented. She wants to talk to me, but not over the phone. She said it was important."

CHAPTER 13

Angie borrowed Jenna's car and made the short drive to the studio apartment in South Coveside. She parked at the curb in front of the landlady's Craftsman-style house. She walked up the porch steps and rang the bell. After a minute passed, the door opened.

"Thanks for coming over." The landlady was a short, plump, sixty-something woman. Her faced looked pinched. "I don't think I introduced myself the last time you were here." She extended her hand. "Marge Hopkins." She gestured for Angie to enter.

The living room was nicely decorated with comfortable blue and white sofas and chairs. Big windows on two sides of the room allowed full sunlight to liven the space. Mrs. Hopkins invited Angie to sit.

"I'm probably making a mountain out of a molehill." She rubbed the side of her face.

"What's bothering you?" Angie couldn't imagine what was causing the woman's distress.

"Since Mrs. Collins left the studio, there have been some odd occurrences." Mrs. Hopkins looked at Angie. "I didn't know the woman or her circumstances, so I didn't know if I should report to the police or not."

"What happened?" Angie sat on the edge of the seat.

"The very evening you moved Mrs. Collins out, a man was lurking near the trees at the end of the driveway near the studio. At first I thought he was with the new tenant, but the new woman in the studio called me. She was alarmed. She reported the man standing there in the dark. She wondered if it was my husband or maybe my son and asked why he was staring at the studio."

"I told her I thought he was with her. I went out on the back porch and he was gone." She shook her head. "I suppose I should have called the police, but I assumed it an isolated incident."

Angie's heart beat quickened. "Was it Tony Collins?"

"I never met the man. I've seen his picture on the news, of course, but that's not the same as seeing someone in person. Mr. Collins rented the studio over the phone. He sent me cash in the mail to pay for the month which I thought was quite odd. Who sends cash by post?" She didn't wait for an answer. "Anyway, it was dark. I couldn't make out the man's features, just his shape and movements." Mrs. Hopkins went on. "If it was Mr. Collins, why wouldn't he just ring the bell and ask me where his wife had gone?"

Thoughts raced through Angie's brain. "Well, if he hit his head and fell overboard, maybe he isn't thinking clearly?"

Mrs. Hopkins' eyebrows knitted together. "If he fell overboard, there's a good chance he's dead."

"Maybe something else is interfering with his thinking. Maybe he had a mild stroke and left the boat after it grounded?"

Mrs. Hopkins pooh-poohed that notion. "Wouldn't someone have found him wandering around by now? Or wouldn't he have asked for help?"

"I don't know," Angie admitted. She weighed the possibility that Tony Collins might have suffered some kind of head injury and somehow was keeping himself hidden from people.

Mrs. Hopkins said, "I don't know these people. I barely spoke to Mrs. Collins when she was here. I don't know what kind of people they are or what they might be mixed up in."

"I don't either," Angie said. "We've been trying to figure this out, but we aren't having much luck."

"Well, there's more. Yesterday, the new renter came to my door. She was livid. She said someone had been in the studio while she was out. She demanded her money back and she was moving out. It took me some time to calm her down. I make my living from my rentals and I can't have poor reviews out on the internet. The locksmith came down last evening and changed the locks."

"Was anything missing from the studio?" Angie wondered if this man had something to do with the Collins's or was just a random nuisance.

"The renter claimed that nothing was missing. She could tell someone had been messing with her stuff though because so many things were out of place." Mrs. Hopkins leaned forward. "I wanted to tell you this because I worry about that poor woman and her little son." She lowered her voice even though she and Angie were the only two people in the house. "I wonder if her husband was mixed up in some trouble. Maybe some creep is trying to find Mr. Collins." Her face darkened. "Or maybe some creep wants to harm Mrs. Collins and the baby."

A shiver of worry ran over Angie's skin.

"I'm going to the police station later today to report all of this," Mrs. Hopkins said. "But I wanted to be sure that Mrs. Collins knew what was going on here in order to keep safe. You know how the police can be, they might not inform her, and really, what can they do? They'll just tell me to call if anything suspicious happens again."

Angie thanked the woman and agreed that reporting the incidents to the police was the right thing to.

As Mrs. Hopkins was walking Angie to the door, she sighed. "It's always something. Why can't there be any peace?"

Exactly. Angie hurried to her car to return the Victorian.

✱✱✱

"WHAT'S COOKIN'?" Courtney asked when Angie came into the kitchen from the back door.

"Plenty." Angie sank onto one of the kitchen chairs.

Mr. Finch sat opposite. He'd been slicing carrots and peppers on the cutting board on the table in front of him. He paused in his task holding the knife in mid-air. "You heard something troubling, Miss Angie?"

"I did." Angie reported the latest news to her three sisters, Mr. Finch, and the cats. Euclid and Circe were resting on top of the fridge and they lifted their heads when Angie arrived in the kitchen.

Courtney added diced tomatoes to the crock pot. She turned, holding the wooden spoon aloft. "So is Tony Collins dead or alive? Is Tony the guy who broke into the studio apartment?"

"I believe that is the pressing question." Mr. Finch put the knife on the table next to the cutting board.

"Is Tony creeping around looking for Deirdre and the baby?" Ellie scowled.

"How are we going to find out if he's alive?" Jenna carried some cut-up baby potatoes to the crock pot.

"Whoever broke into the studio apartment must have been looking for Deirdre," Angie said. "Now he knows she isn't staying there any more. What will he do next?" She sniffed the air. "What are you making? It smells great."

Courtney added vegetable broth to the pot. "We made vegetable lasagna for dinner. It's in the oven. It will be ready in ten minutes. We're making a vegetable stew for tomorrow."

"I'm starving." Angie took a slice of red pepper off of Mr. Finch's cutting board.

"This is one strange case." Jenna removed a salad from the refrigerator. "Patrick Ackerman was on the Collins's boat and his body washed up, but he could have fallen overboard. There might not be any foul play involved with his death." She let out an exasperated sigh. "And we don't know if Tony has met with foul play, is alive, or is dead because of an accident."

"Why don't you talk to Louisa?" Ellie washed her hands in the sink. "She was on Marion Island with Tony. Maybe she can tell us something."

Angie made a face. "Ugh. I really don't want to tell Louisa we know she was on the island with Tony. She'll get defensive. She'll think we're judging her. Then we won't get any useful information."

"You could approach the subject tactfully," Mr. Finch suggested.

Angie groaned. "How?" She looked at Ellie. "You ask her. You're always tactful. You have a nice way of talking to people."

Ellie placed slices of garlic bread in a basket. "Don't think you can sweet-talk me into doing it. You and Jenna have already discussed Tony with Louisa. It would seem odd for me to butt in now. Your conversation would be a natural progression from what she told you previously."

Angie put her chin in her hand and looked at Ellie. "How do you do that? How do you get out of doing things by making sense?"

Everybody chuckled.

"What's wrong with our powers?" Angie asked. "Why can't one of us just conjure up an image of the crime scene? Why can't we just picture the killer in our brains?"

"Oooh." Courtney glanced over at Angie. "That might be something worth trying."

"I don't think that's possible." Jenna removed the lasagna from the oven which filled the kitchen with a delicious aroma.

As Ellie was taking plates from the cabinet, she moaned. "Why do we always get interrupted at dinner time?"

The others turned to her with questioning looks.

"Why are you saying that?" Angie asked.

The front doorbell rang.

Everyone stared at Ellie with their mouths hanging open.

CHAPTER 14

Courtney turned away from the counter and eyed Ellie. "Since you knew the doorbell was about to ring, would you also like to tell us who is standing on the porch?"

Ellie blinked. "What do you mean?"

Angie stood up. "You knew someone was going to ring the bell."

"No, I didn't." Ellie looked at her sisters like they were crazy.

"Miss Ellie," Finch began. "You sensed our dinner was about to be interrupted?"

"You said those very words." Jenna moved closer to Ellie. "You said something about dinner being interrupted."

Ellie shook her head. "Maybe I said something else, something that sounded like that." She scowled. "I don't recall saying anything at all."

The door bell sounded again.

"I'll go." Angie moved to the hallway with the two cats trailing behind. When she got to the foyer she reached for the knob and pulled the door open.

Louisa from the Coveside coffee shop stood on the porch. She was wearing jeans and a navy tank top and the blue ends of her hair rested over her shoulders.

Angie's eyebrows raised in surprise.

"Hey." Louisa looked shy or sheepish. "Can I talk to you for a minute?"

"Sure." Angie stepped back so the young woman could enter.

Louisa gazed about the foyer noting the wide carved wooden staircase, the beautiful wood floors, and lovely décor. "Wow, this is beautiful."

Angie thanked her. "Is everything okay?"

Louisa was glancing around at the two rooms off the foyer. "Oh, yeah. Everything's fine."

Angie waited to hear the reason Louisa had shown up on their doorstep.

Louisa cleared her throat. "I heard you've been interviewing for help to work in your new bake shop."

Angie tilted her head.

"If the positions aren't all filled, could I interview with you?" Louisa nervously grasped her hands together in front of her.

"You're leaving the coffee shop in Coveside?" Angie was surprised that Louisa had plans to leave her job. She'd been a fixture there for a few years. "You've been there forever."

"It's time for a change." Louisa shrugged one shoulder.

"Why don't we sit on the porch?" The family would be coming into the dining room to eat dinner at any moment and Angie wanted to have some privacy. She opened the door and led Louisa to the small glass table and chairs. "Want something to drink?"

The young woman declined and sank into the soft cushion of the porch chair. "What a great porch. I love it."

Angie sat down across from her. "Why do you want to leave the coffee shop?"

Louisa turned her head to watch the people walking by on the sidewalk. "It's hectic down there."

"It's hectic in my shop, too." Angie wondered what Louisa meant. Was Louisa burnt out? If so, working in the bake shop wouldn't provide a slower pace.

"Oh, I know." Louisa turned back to Angie clearly concerned she was giving the wrong impression. "You're place was always really popular and busy."

Angie got the sense that Louisa wasn't being upfront about her reasons for leaving her present job. "Did you have a falling out with the owner or something?"

Louisa's eyes widened. The pitch of her voice got slightly higher. "No, nothing like that. Jack and I get along fine. He doesn't even know I'm thinking of giving notice."

Angie sat quietly waiting for her to explain.

Louisa let out a long sigh. "I want to change jobs because I think the atmosphere and clientele will be different at your place."

"How do you mean?"

"There are a lot of guys who come into Coveside. I'm the only woman working in the coffee shop. The guys can get boisterous." Louisa's face clouded. "Sometimes they're disrespectful." She waved her hand. "I know it's all just high spirits and lots of testosterone flowing and most of them mean well."

"But?" Angie questioned.

"But some of them think I'm only there to flirt with them. Sometimes they say things to me that I don't appreciate." She looked at Angie. "I'm looking for a different atmosphere, a place where I don't get stared at or have rude comments made to me. If I get annoyed by their antics down at Coveside, well, then I get teased for being a witch." She shook her head. "I've just had enough. I'd like the chance to work with other women and with a less rowdy group of customers."

Angie knew that Louisa was a good worker and she could use someone experienced in her new shop. She felt wary though because of the young woman's interactions with Tony Collins. She also wondered if she could trust her since the sisters' had concerns that Louisa could have been involved in Tony's disappearance. Angie had to bring the subject up. She sucked in a deep breath. "You know when Jenna and I stopped at the coffee shop the other day? You mentioned that Tony Collins had flirted with you?"

Louisa's posture became rigid. "Yeah?"

"So Jenna and Courtney and I were on Marion Island recently." Angie hoped that Louisa would say something about being there, but she remained silent. Angie decided to allow the silence between them to linger. After a few moments, Louisa said, "Did you have a good time?"

"We didn't go there to enjoy ourselves." Angie waited.

"Then why did you go there?"

"We went to see if we could find out anything about Tony Collins."

"Like what? Why?"

"Because we have Mrs. Collins living here with us."

Louisa's eyebrows went up. "She is? What does she say about her husband?"

"Not a whole lot." A sudden sense of weariness washed over Angie. She wished people would stop holding back information and tell the truth. "I don't think she's telling us everything she knows."

Louisa squirmed a bit in her seat. "She must be in a terrible state over Tony's disappearance."

"I think she's in some sort of state of shock. She doesn't say a lot about her husband. It's a little surprising." Angie wanted to draw Louisa into conversation about Tony to see if she would admit anything. She knew it was a long shot.

"Maybe she didn't like him much." Louisa sat back in her chair.

Angie feigned surprise. "Why do you say that?"

"Maybe she figured out that her dear husband was unfaithful." There was an edge to Louisa's tone.

"How do you know he wasn't faithful? Just because of his flirting?" Angie held the young woman's eyes.

"Because he was a jerk." Louisa looked like she wanted to spit.

"Do you know more?" Angie's heart was pounding. She wanted to shout at Louisa to tell her what she knew, but she kept her voice neutral. "Why is he a jerk?"

Louisa's posture relaxed and she shook her head. "I didn't know he was married. He asked me out. He asked me to meet him on Marion Island. Tony said he was going there to meet with some business associate. He told me to take the ferry over and we could meet for lunch and walk around." She ran her hands through her hair. "So I did."

"Was this the day Tony went missing?"

"Yeah. I went there. It seemed so glamorous to go to the island and meet a handsome man for lunch."

"So you met him?"

"We had a nice lunch. We got ice cream and

walked around. He asked if I'd like to see his boat, so we went down to the docks. He had told me to bring a swimsuit. I had it in my bag. Tony suggested I put it on and we could sunbathe on the deck for a while. Have a glass of wine before his appointment." Color rose in Louisa's cheeks. "I went below to change. I'd forgotten to bring sunscreen so I called up to Tony to ask if he had any. He said to look in his backpack." Anger stiffened her jaw. "I saw a backpack on the floor and looked inside." Louisa's eyes flashed. "I didn't find the sunscreen, but I found something else. Rohypnol."

Angie looked blank.

"A date rape drug."

Angie opened her mouth to speak, but nothing came out.

"Tony Dear must have had something planned with me. The drug knocks people out, like a sedative. Then they can't fight back when ... well, you can imagine the rest."

"What did you do?" Angie asked in a small voice.

"I stormed away," Louisa said. "I told the jerk that something important had come up."

Angie blinked. "That's awful. What an awful person."

"Wouldn't you love to be married to a gem like that?" Louisa shook her head. "I didn't know he was married." She let out a chuckle. "Before I went below deck, Tony said his *sister* and her son were visiting with him. He said that's whose toys and stuff were down there. I believed him. His *sister*. God."

"What did you do after leaving his boat?"

"I practically ran to the ferry office. I bought a ticket and went home. I was so angry, Angie, I could have killed him." She realized how her words sounded and her mouth hung open. "I mean, I didn't...."

Angie nodded. "I know what you meant."

"It's just a figure of speech." Louisa looked worried that Angie might think she did something to Tony Collins. "I would never do anything to hurt anyone." She paused for a few seconds. "Even someone I think deserves it."

Angie glanced at the cats. They sat staring at Louisa, but neither one hissed or arched their back or seemed wary of the young woman.

Angie decided that she was inclined to believe what Louisa had just told her.

CHAPTER 15

Angie went into the house and found her sisters and Mr. Finch sitting together in the family room. Euclid jumped onto the sofa and settled next to Jenna and Courtney. Circe leaped onto Mr. Finch's lap and curled up as the older man stroked her soft velvet fur. Ellie was sitting in an easy chair reading and when Angie came in she lifted her head from the book. "I made you a plate with lasagna and garlic bread and put it in the fridge."

Courtney had snuck into the hall after Angie went to answer the door to listen to find out who had rung the bell. She reported to the family and they decided to eat dinner in the family room in case Angie needed privacy to speak with the unexpected visitor. Courtney eyed her sister. "What was the evening visit about?" She scratched Euclid's cheeks and he purred.

Angie told them what she and Louisa had discussed.

"Drugs?" Ellie nearly screeched. "Tony Collins was going to drug Louisa? What a terrible man."

Her face was screwed up from equal parts disgust and disbelief.

"It's not that unusual." Jenna scowled. "Guys mix it into a drink and then the woman becomes a submissive partner."

"Sometimes the woman doesn't even remember it happened." Courtney was fuming.

"I have a thought." Mr. Finch looked at the girls. "It is a twist on the possible use of the drug."

The girls gave Finch their full attention.

"I wonder if perhaps Mr. Collins did not intend to drug Miss Louisa at all." He continued to run his hand over Circe's smooth fur. "I wonder if Mr. Collins used the drug to sedate his wife."

"What?" Ellie's eyes were as wide as saucers. "Why would he do that?"

Finch explained his thought. "What if Mr. Collins had ill intent, but his misdeed was planned for Mr. Ackerman?"

Courtney leaned forward. "Brilliant." She smiled at Finch. "Tony used the drug to sedate Deirdre so he could kill Patrick Ackerman with her on the boat, but without her knowledge." Courtney winked at Finch. "Watching our crime shows has turned you into a master detective, Mr. Finch."

Angie looked pensive. "That could be right." She turned to Jenna and Courtney. "Remember how odd Deirdre seemed when she got off the boat? She was sort of glassy-eyed and slow-moving. She seemed very disoriented, slow to react. She claimed she'd had a migraine, but maybe she had been drugged."

"That's a very interesting possibility." Jenna got up and picked up her laptop. "I'm going to look up the side effects of that drug. See if Deirdre's behavior could be related to having ingested it." She tapped on her keyboard.

Ellie fiddled with the ends of her long blonde hair. "But."

The others looked at her.

"But what?" Courtney asked.

"But why would Tony disappear if he had made a plan like that?" Ellie's forehead was creased from confusion. "If he drugged Deirdre to keep her out of the way while he killed Ackerman, then he would have an alibi. Not iron-clad, but an alibi. Deirdre would vouch that she was on the boat with Tony and that she heard nothing. She said she isn't even sure that Ackerman was still on the boat when they got underway. Since she was drugged and unconscious, Deirdre can claim that she never heard a fight. So if Tony has an alibi, why did he take off?"

Finch and the sisters were quiet trying to think of a reason that Tony would flee.

"Maybe the fact that the alibi was not iron-clad worried him and he decided to run away," Jenna offered.

"Tony could have fallen overboard during the fight with Ackerman," Courtney proposed.

Finch rubbed his chin in thought. "I wonder why Mr. Collins would want Ackerman dead? What could have been his motive? Has Chief Martin suggested a reason?"

Angie said, "No, at least he hasn't told us why Tony might have wanted Ackerman dead. He only mentioned a business deal between the two."

"Maybe the motive doesn't matter for us." Jenna peered at the laptop screen. "Ackerman's dead. Either Tony did it or Ackerman fell off the boat. Knowing *why* Tony might want him dead doesn't really help us figure out where Tony is or what happened to him." Jenna tapped again. "Here's the information on the drug. Deirdre's odd behavior and flat expression can be after-effects of taking that drug." Jenna looked up from her screen. "Although, having had a migraine can leave a person with the same side-effects."

"Ugh." Ellie moaned. "We're spinning our wheels. There are too many possibilities."

"What about the guy who was lurking around at the studio apartment?" Angie curled her legs up under her. "We haven't really talked about that."

"Let's discuss possibilities." Courtney lifted her hand with her index finger pointing up. "One ... it was Tony Collins looking for Deirdre." Another finger went up. "Two ... it was someone else."

Jenna shook her head at her sister's joke. "Two ... it was a member of the media looking for a story."

124

Ellie looked aghast. "A member of the media wouldn't break into an apartment."

"Really, Sis?" Courtney raised an eyebrow. "Unfortunately, not everyone in the world shares your sense of right and wrong."

"Who else could have been looking for Deirdre?" Jenna placed her laptop on the coffee table. "Someone she made friends with down at the docks?"

Angie offered her opinion. "A casual acquaintance wouldn't break into the apartment."

Mr. Finch spoke. "Perhaps someone is trying to find Mr. Collins, not Mrs. Collins. Maybe it was someone who wants revenge on Mr. Collins for the death of Mr. Ackerman?"

"That's a good point." Ellie's voice trembled. Her face was pale and she gave a shudder. "So many awful people."

Courtney shifted in her seat. "We really need to question Deirdre about what she knows. We've been dancing around her too much because we feel bad for her being left alone with a baby. We need to ask her some hard questions and see how she responds." She narrowed her eyes. "I can't shake the thought that she is guilty. I don't know if she murdered her husband, but she was up to something on that boat."

Angie blew out a breath. "Then we need to find out what it was that she was up to. Maybe that will lead us to other answers."

"Well, we better talk to her soon." Jenna closed her laptop down. "The police will release the boat and car to her any day now. She'll probably sell the boat right away. As soon as she gets a means of transportation and some money, she'll be out of here."

"Lack of money is the only reason she's still in town." Ellie agreed. "If Tony's body washes up and she gets a death certificate, then she'll have access to Tony's bank account and away she'll go."

Angie turned to Mr. Finch. "I wonder if you could hold something of Deirdre's. Maybe you could sense what she's hiding. Or what she's guilty of."

"I would certainly be willing to try." Finch nodded. "Perhaps when she takes her son in the yard to play I could go outside to sit in the garden and talk to her."

"Good idea," Ellie said. "I'll keep watch when I'm in the kitchen and I'll text you when I see them out there."

Angie's phone beeped with a text message. "It's Chief Martin. He says he's going to Aunt Anna's place and wants to know if any of us can join him. He'd like us to walk around, take another look in the barn to see if we can pick up on any clues about who put the beds in the hayloft."

"Sounds good to me." Courtney stood up. "There are only crime show reruns on tonight anyway." She smiled at Finch. "Come on, Mr.

Finch. Let's put our detecting abilities to work."

Finch gently moved Circe to the side, pushed himself out of the chair, and reached for his cane. "I will do my best."

"Let's all go." Jenna looked at Ellie. "You come too."

A look of horror washed over Ellie's face. She started to protest, but Jenna cut her off. "There's nothing to be afraid of. We're just going to look at the barn. We could use your insight."

Ellie reluctantly got up.

Circe jumped down from the chair just as Euclid stretched and stepped off the sofa to follow everyone out of the room.

Jenna picked up her purse. "By the way, Angie. What did you tell Louisa about the job she wants at your bake shop?"

"I hired her."

CHAPTER 16

The Roselands, Mr. Finch, Chief Martin, and the cats loaded themselves into Ellie's van and she drove to Anna's house. Chief Martin left his vehicle at the Victorian. Anna was standing on the front porch with her arms wrapped around herself when they pulled into the driveway and she stepped down the stairs to greet them. The sun was setting behind the trees and shadows were gathering in the backyard. Anna was introduced to Ellie and Mr. Finch.

"I could barely keep myself from having Jacob remove those items from the hayloft." Anna had a scowl on her face. "It's almost a feeling of violation having someone on my property without my permission using my barn for their own purposes. This is my home."

Chief Martin took Anna's arm. "I just thought we should take another look before you have the things removed. Just in case we can figure something out by having another look. After tonight, go ahead and have Jacob throw the things

128

away."

Anna looked down at the cats. "At least you brought those dear animals with you. They always make me feel better."

Hearing the praise, Euclid puffed himself up and trilled.

Leading the group to the barn, Anna asked, "Do some of you have police training? Is that why you're helping Phillip?"

Everyone shared quick glances. Angie was happy to let Chief Martin explain the presence of so many people and she remained quiet waiting to hear what he might come up with.

"Well, the girls have some experience in investigation," the chief said as they crossed the lawn.

"We haven't been formally trained," Ellie told Anna. "We've sort of just fallen into it on a very limited basis."

"How interesting." Anna looked like she was about to ask more questions when Mr. Finch spoke to distract her. "I've just come along as a family friend."

"How do you know the girls?" Anna took Mr. Finch's elbow as they walked over an uneven part of the lawn.

"I live in the house behind them." Finch didn't want to explain that he'd met the girls when his brother had been murdered several months ago.

"Mr. Finch is part of our family." Ellie smiled.

"I don't know what we'd do without him."

Finch leaned close to Anna and whispered. "These four sisters give me far more than I could ever give them." The man peeked over the rim of his glasses and winked. "But don't tell them I said that."

When they reached the barn, Anna opened the door and flicked on the lights. Looking at the ladder to the hayloft, she let out a sigh.

Chief Martin led Courtney, Jenna, and Ellie up the ladder. Angie told them that she would stay on the ground floor with Anna and Mr. Finch. Somehow the cats found a way up before the humans could reach the loft. Euclid and Circe's little faces stared down at the people as they climbed up the ladder. When everyone reached the top, they stepped away from the edge of the loft and disappeared from view, but the three remaining in the main part of the barn heard Ellie let out a gasp of surprise when she saw the setup.

Chief Martin came over to the ladder with a blanket in his hands. "This is from one of the beds. I'll drop it to you."

The blanket floated down to them and Angie caught it. She handed it off to Mr. Finch who hooked his cane over his arm and carefully took hold of the blanket. Angie watched his face for a moment.

Footsteps scuffed over the heavy old wooden floor of the loft as the three girls and the chief walked around the space looking for any clues about who had placed the things up there. After ten minutes, they each stepped slowly down the rungs.

"Did you see anything of use?" Anna looked hopeful.

"Not really." The chief shook his head and took another glance up at the loft. "Will Jacob remove the things for you? If not, I'll come back tomorrow and get rid of them."

Anna waved her hand. "Jacob will take care of it for me. You don't need to do it." She started to lead the group from the barn.

Angie was about to follow, when a zing of little electric sparks danced over her skin. She took a look at Courtney to see if she might have felt the same thing, but her sister seemed unaffected.

Jenna was about to call for the cats when she saw them moving towards the door. "How did you two get down here so fast?"

As they crossed the lawn, Angie sidled next to Anna. "Has Jacob worked for you for a long time?"

"Oh, no. Maybe a month and a half. I was lucky to find such a good worker."

"Is he from Sweet Cove?" Angie felt the need to find out some things about the gardener.

"No, he said he'd grown up in a small town in Vermont. He learned landscaping from his grandfather." Anna smiled. "He does very nice work."

"How did you find him?"

"He knocked on my door one day. He said he was new to town and was starting a landscaping business. He gave me his flyer."

The electric zing pulsed over Angie's skin again. While Anna chattered on about Jacob's skills and the way he wasn't afraid of hard work, Angie zoned out trying to understand what her senses were trying to tell her.

***

BACK IN the van, Chief Martin sat in the second row of seats and leaned a bit forward towards Finch who was sitting in the front passenger seat with Circe on his lap on the folded blanket from the hayloft. "So, anything, Mr. Finch?"

Finch scratched the black cat's cheek. "I sense the person who prepared the loft with the items."

Although Ellie was driving, she took a quick glance at Finch. Her knuckles were white from gripping the wheel so tightly.

"It is one person. A man. I sense the preparation was done for someone else. But I discern a failed purpose."

"Things didn't work out?" Angie looked out the van window at the darkened streets of Sweet Cove. "That's why everything seemed unused."

"Who the heck did it?" Courtney sat in the third row with Euclid between her and Jenna.

Angie reported how she sensed something when

Anna talked about Jacob.

"Does he know something?" Jenna asked. "Did he see someone?"

"If he did, why wouldn't he tell Anna?" Ellie held tight to the steering wheel.

"Maybe he was threatened to keep quiet," Courtney suggested. "Maybe the person threatened to hurt Anna if Jacob told anyone."

Chief Martin strained in his seat to look back at Courtney. "Do you get a feeling that Aunt Anna is in danger?"

Courtney was quiet for a moment. "I don't, no."

"We need to talk to Jacob." Angie couldn't shake the feeling that the young man knew something. Zings picked at her skin. "Can we turn back and drive over to that sitting area next to the trolley stop behind Anna's house? I feel like we need to go there."

Ellie pulled over to the edge of the road and swung the van back in the direction they'd just come from. In five minutes, she steered the van to the curb and parked just beyond the tiny park with the granite memorial and everyone emerged from the vehicle.

They walked around under the street lamp inspecting the space. After a minute of moving about, Angie sat down on one of the benches and took slow, deep breaths. She closed her eyes trying to pick up on sensations floating on the air.

When she lifted her lids, her eyes focused on the

building set diagonally across from the park. It was a big rambling old house. The place was well-tended and had flowers planted around the edges of the building. A large floral wreath hung on the front door. Angie squinted in the darkness. There seemed to be a barn slightly behind the home with a stone walkway leading to it. A carved wooden sign hung from a post and small light bulbs shined on the words, *Francine's Stained Glass Studio.*

Angie turned her head to look at the grove of trees growing on the property line between the park and Anna's back yard. She shifted her gaze to the house across the street trying to determine the line of sight. Angie stood up. "We need to talk to the Francine who owns that house."

"Yeah," Courtney said following her sister's gaze. "I feel it, too."

The two cats trilled in agreement.

CHAPTER 17

It was too late to go knocking on someone's door, so the group returned to the Victorian and in the morning, after the B and B breakfast rush, Angie, Jenna, and Courtney drove back to the edge of Sweet Cove and pulled into the small gravel lot off the driveway of *Francine's Stained Glass Studio*. Ellie stayed behind to take care of business and Mr. Finch was taking the morning shift in the candy store. The girls didn't think it was a good idea to take the cats to a stained glass store, so they left them at home and received much hissing and scowling from Euclid when he found out he couldn't go.

"Have you ever been in this shop?" Courtney eyed the pretty blue door with the huge floral wreath hanging on it. A pot filled with flowers stood on each step. The place looked well-cared for and welcoming.

"Never. I didn't even know it was here." Jenna opened the door and held it for her sisters to enter.

The shop had wide pine floorboards and the

walls had been painted a soothing butter cream. Shelves and hangers displayed various objects made from stained glass. The glass pieces in the Tiffany style lamps caught the light and sparkled. Several stained glass window panels made of hundreds of intricately placed pale blue and yellow glass pieces were displayed over the shop's windows.

An attractive, slender, middle-aged woman with shoulder-length blonde hair stood at a work table near one of the windows moving different colored pieces of glass around to create an abstract design. She wore jeans and a lavender blouse with the sleeves rolled up.

The woman looked up when the girls came in and she gave them a warm smile. After wiping her hands on a towel, she moved to greet the sisters. "Welcome. I'm Francine." The woman's skin was flawless and her green eyes sparkled like shimmering pieces of emerald glass. "Is there anything special you're looking for or would you just like to browse?"

Angie returned her smile. "We're just browsing really. Your things are exquisite."

Courtney and Jenna were moving up and down the aisles mesmerized by the lovely objects.

"Yesterday, we were visiting an acquaintance over on Suomi Street and when we were leaving, we saw your shop. We decided to come back today to look around." Angie lifted a small jeweled box and held it up to the light. "Do you make everything yourself?"

"I do. I've been creating stained glass designs for about twenty-five years. After I opened the studio, everything took off. I can barely keep up with my commissions." Francine explained her background and how she got started with the business. She had a infectious laugh and a bubbly personality. "I really could use an assistant, but it would be hard to find the time to train someone."

Angie liked the woman. She seemed like someone who would make a wonderful friend.

"Who do you know over on Suomi Street?" Francine asked.

"Anna Lincoln."

"Anna's a great person." Francine smiled. "Sometimes I meet her and a group of regulars at the coffee shop in the mornings. Anna does beautiful quilting work. She's quite the artist."

Angie glanced out one of the windows. "I was sitting over at the little memorial park the other day. I noticed that you probably had a nice view of the spot from your shop."

"When I work at my table, I have a direct view of the park." Francine tilted her head and studied Angie for several seconds. "Is there something you want to ask me?"

Angie swallowed and tried to sound nonchalant. "Have you ever noticed anything unusual happening over there?"

Francine's soft bangs were brushed to one side. Her eyes narrowed slightly in a questioning expression. "How do you mean?"

"Some objects have been placed on Anna's property recently. We all wondered how they got there." Angie was trying to be as vague as possible. "Then we noticed that Anna's property line abutted the park and we thought maybe the things were brought in through the trees from that direction." She gestured towards the park.

Francine picked up on Angie's intentional vagueness and didn't press for more details. She pursed her lips and gently tapped a finger to her chin. "I've been working very late the past couple of weeks."

Angie's heart sank. She thought that Francine was probably too engrossed in her work to have seen anything going on near the park.

"The town maintenance department takes care of the trolley stop and the memorial park. They mow the little strip of lawn, plant and tend the flowers. They park in that gravel section on the other side of the bushes there." Francine moved to one of the windows and bent slightly. "See." She pointed.

Angie stood beside her and leaned forward to look out the window. She nodded.

Francine continued. "One night, I saw a van pull in there. Someone got out and removed a good sized bin from the rear of the truck. The way he moved gave me the impression he was a younger man. I couldn't describe his features ... it was too dark and he was too far away. I wondered what the guy was doing at the park so late."

"What did he do with the bin?" Jenna had come up behind Angie and Francine.

Francine adjusted her stance to include Jenna in the conversation. "He carried the bin behind the benches. Then I couldn't see him anymore. It was dark and he stepped out of the light. I figured there must be a maintenance box or some such thing where the workers kept gardening supplies. I thought the man must be stocking the box." She shrugged.

"Was the truck parked there long?" Courtney had pulled herself away from browsing and stood next to Jenna.

"I don't know. I went back to my work. I forgot about the truck. It seemed odd for a maintenance man to be there at that hour, but I just thought the guy was working late." Francine adjusted a few items on a shelf and then looked at the girls. "Did the man do something he shouldn't have?"

Jenna shook her head. "We don't really know. We're looking for some link in order to explain how the items got placed on Anna's property."

"You don't want to share what those items are?" Francine was pretty sure the sisters preferred to keep that part of the story to themselves.

Courtney raised a shoulder and shook her head.

"I understand." Francine remembered something and her green eyes widened. "Oh, you know what? That van came back again another night, maybe two nights after the first time I saw it. It was late again, quite dark. The man got out. This time he carried a metal box. It looked sort of like a metal tool case. It reflected the light of the streetlamp." She rubbed the back of her neck. "I ignored him. I thought it was just a town worker taking care of something." Her lips turned down. "He was up to no good?"

"Maybe." Angie wasn't sure how much, if anything, they should share with Francine. What they'd heard was interesting information and even though Francine hadn't seen the man with anything large like a twin mattress, she may have been focused on her work or was in another part of the house when the beds were moved through the trees and into Anna's barn.

Angie thanked Francine for her help and as she turned to leave, Jenna picked up a small lamp made with different shades of blue and rose stained glass. She grinned. "I'm going to get this for my jewelry shop."

Francine rang up the sale and carefully wrapped and packaged the lamp. When the girls were going out the door, Courtney stopped and looked back at Francine. "What color was the van?"

"It was white."

"Was anything written on the sides? A company

name? The town logo?"

"Nothing," Francine said.

A plain white van. Angie's heart started to beat double-time.

CHAPTER 18

When the girls were back in the car, Angie rubbed her forehead. "It must be Anna's gardener. Jacob must have put the beds in the barn."

Courtney held Jenna's package with the lamp in it. "When Francine said it was a white van, I felt the humming in my blood." Whenever danger was near or something was off, Angie and Courtney could feel a thrumming in their bodies. Their grandmother had also experienced the same sensation which the girls considered a sort of early warning system. Some people might say it was just a hyper-strong sense of intuition, but the sisters believed it was much more than that and for the past few months, they'd been trying to train themselves to be more aware of the signals.

Something popped into Angie's mind and she turned to her sisters. "When we were at Anna's, I asked Jacob what was on the other side of the trees. He said he'd never gone behind the trees so he didn't know. Then when we were going through the wooded section to take a look, he told us there was nothing to see." A look of anger played over Angie's face as she remembered the incident. "He lied. He knew very well what was on the other side of the trees."

The girls discussed Jacob's episode of deceit until Jenna pulled the car into the Victorian's driveway. They got out and walked up the stairs to the porch just as Ellie and the cats came out of the house. Ellie carried a watering can. "Did you get any answers from the stained glass woman?"

Angie told her what they'd learned. The cats hissed.

Courtney frowned. "What is Jacob up to? Is he living in Anna's barn sometimes?"

"Does he take women there at night?" Jenna was disgusted that Jacob had the nerve to make a place for himself in Anna's barn. "What an entitled jerk. That's Anna's home. He has no right to infringe on her property, make her feel unsafe in her own house."

Ellie let out a sigh of contempt as she tipped the watering can to the pot of white and pink flowers. "Well, you'd better talk to Chief Martin. Tell him your concerns."

Angie's phone buzzed with an incoming text. She took a look at the screen and then stared at Ellie. "You just did it again."

Ellie blinked in confusion. "Huh?"

Angie held up her phone. "The text is from Chief Martin."

Ellie looked puzzled.

"You mentioned Chief Martin a moment before the text came in. This is the third time you've mentioned someone's name or that something was going to happen, and then a second later, it does."

Courtney grinned. "Wow, you're developing a new skill."

Ellie's face muscles drooped and she stammered nervously. "I ... I.... it's a coincidence." She busied herself with watering the flower pots. "It's just a coincidence, that's all." The three sisters could see Ellie's hands shaking.

"Don't get freaked out." Courtney smiled. "It's cool."

Ellie shook her head causing her blonde locks to fall forward. "There isn't anything cool about not having control over one's self."

Courtney sat in one of the porch rockers. "I'd like to be able to do what you can do."

"I'd be happy to pass the skills over to you." Ellie pouted as she moved to the next group of flowers.

"Have you been practicing your telekinesis?" Courtney asked. "That is the best of all of our skills." Ellie had once turned a gun into a soft pretzel-shaped piece of rubber in order to save her sisters, Mr. Finch, and Euclid. The realization that she could do such a thing scared her nearly to death. Courtney had been encouraging Ellie to hone her ability and a few weeks ago, Ellie had been able to make a spoon float in the air for several seconds.

"No, I've been too busy." Ellie had a difficult time accepting that such things were possible and even though she'd been excited on the night when she'd made the spoon float, she quickly became frightened and uneasy about her gifts. She preferred to hide from it and pretend that she didn't have any paranormal abilities.

"Embrace who you are, Sis," Courtney told her. "Don't run from it."

Jenna sat down next to Courtney and rocked. "By the way, I happen to think that *my* skill is the best one of all of ours." Jenna could sometimes see the spirits of those who had passed. On the last case they'd been involved with, she'd seen fleeting images of a murder taking place.

Courtney considered. "Yeah. Your thing is pretty cool, too."

"So what does the chief say in his text?" Jenna asked.

"The boat is ready to be released to Mrs. Collins. But before that happens, he wants us to come down to the dock and go on board." Angie looked at Ellie. "He'd like all of us to come."

The color drained from Ellie's face.

"But he understands if you don't feel up to it." Angie gave Ellie an understanding look.

Ellie just fiddled with the flowers and didn't say anything.

"Is there employee coverage at the candy store?" Angie asked Courtney. "Mr. Finch should come along, too."

Courtney nodded. "There are two other people on for this shift. We're putting more people on when Mr. Finch is working in case he gets too tired." The girls and Finch's girlfriend were making sure that Finch didn't overdo since he'd been bopped over the head and knocked unconscious during their last case. "He wouldn't want to miss going to the boat. I'll text him."

Angie checked the time. "There's an hour before we have to meet the chief. Let's go inside and do an internet search on Jacob."

"I can just do the search on my phone." Jenna reached for it.

"I need to eat something." Angie opened the door and the cats strolled into the foyer. "Let's make lunch and look him up at the same time." The girls gathered in the kitchen where they warmed up leftover curry chicken and vegetable stew. Ellie removed a fruit salad from the fridge.

Jenna sat at the kitchen table with her laptop. "What's Jacob's last name?"

Everyone had a blank look on their faces.

Courtney thought about whether or not they'd been told the gardener's last name when they were introduced. "We never heard. Did we?"

Angie headed for the back door. "I'll call Anna and ask her." She stepped out to the patio and made the call to find out the information. As she was clicking off from Aunt Anna, Deirdre came around the corner of the house from the driveway pushing Brendan in a stroller. She startled when she saw Angie standing a few yards away. "Oh, hi."

Angie said hello and smiled. She had a hundred questions for Deirdre, but she knew the woman would get spooked if she started to interrogate her. She decided to tackle that task just before Chief Martin released the boat to her. "How are you doing?"

Deirdre handed Brendan a fluffy toy puppy. "I'm better. I feel better. Thanks so much for letting us use the apartment for a few days. I'll pay you back. I promise."

Angie waved her hand. "Don't worry about it. I'm glad we could help."

Brendan brought the toy puppy up to his face and chattered away to it. A green fleece material covered his chubby little legs and when the youngster started kicking his feet as if he were running, the blanket fell off his lap.

Angie bent to pick it up.

"Oh, that's my sweatshirt." Deirdre reached for the pullover. "Brendan loves the feel of the cloth." She tied it around her waist and Angie could see the words "Columbia University" written across the fabric.

"Did you go to Columbia?" Angie asked.

Deirdre blinked. "What? Oh, no. I bought the

sweatshirt a long time ago when we visited New York."

The two women talked for a few minutes and then Deirdre lifted her son from the stroller. "I'm going to bring Brendan in for lunch and a nap now. Nice to see you." She and her baby disappeared into the carriage house.

Angie returned to the kitchen where Jenna and Ellie sat at the table eating their lunch. Courtney perched on a stool at the island. There was a bowl of veggie stew and a small dish of fruit salad on the counter beside her. Courtney pointed. "I made you a bowl. What took so long to make the call?"

Angie told them that she'd run into Deirdre out in the yard and that they'd exchanged a few pleasantries.

Courtney lifted her spoon to her mouth and paused. "That woman knows something. I can feel it."

Angie also reported on her phone call. "Aunt Anna says that Jacob's last name is Littlefield. Remember someone said he'd moved down from Vermont?" She started in on her stew.

Jenna's fingers flew over the keyboard of her laptop. She chuckled. "A bunch of things come up about a Jacob Littlefield from the 1800s. I don't think he's our man."

"Does Jacob have a website for his business?" Ellie asked.

"Nothing so far." Jenna squinted at the screen

for a few minutes. "There's nothing. No business site, no social media for him, no nothing." She looked up. "Isn't that odd?"

"That's impossible." Courtney got up and went to Jenna's laptop. She tapped for a minute and then straightened. "Is this guy a ghost? Because there isn't anything about him online."

"Figures." Angie groaned. "The bake shop is opening soon. I have so much to do. I don't have time to look into all of this." Her shoulders slumped. "I guess we'll have to go talk to him the next time he's working at Anna's."

"Don't worry. We'll help you get the shop ready." Jenna looked at her sister. "We stick together."

Ellie rinsed her plate and put it in the dishwasher. "It's a good thing we stick together. You better stick with me when we get on that boat." Her voice trembled at the thought of visiting a possible crime scene. "Let's get this over with."

The girls were amazed that Ellie had decided to go along, but they didn't mention their surprise to her. They finished eating, cleaned up, and grabbed their things. Heading out the back door to Ellie's van, the cats paraded after them.

"Don't let me get scared." Ellie whispered to Jenna and clutched her arm.

"Too late. You're already scared." Courtney swung her arm over Ellie's shoulder and hugged her. "Don't worry, Sis. We've got your back."

They piled into the van, picked Mr. Finch up at the candy store, and headed down Main Street to the harbor. There was no conversation as they traveled. An anticipatory anxiousness had fallen over them and each person's focus was on what they might discover on the boat.

CHAPTER 19

Ellie parked the van in the harbor lot and they piled out and walked to the harbor master's office where Chief Martin was waiting for them. Ellie carried Circe in her arms and patted the black cat's head which seemed to lessen her fears about being on the boat. Mr. Finch leaned on his cane and Euclid walked beside him, his giant orange plume held high.

The harbor master was a gray-haired, slight man with a deep, dark tan. He raised his bushy gray eyebrows when he saw the animals. "Cats?"

"They accompany the girls." The chief hoped his obscure comment would puzzle the man and would keep him from asking any more questions. "Is the boat still in the same slip?"

The man nodded. "I hope Mrs. Collins moves it out of here soon. There are too many gawkers coming around who want to see the missing man's boat." He frowned and returned to his paperwork.

Chief Martin led the way to the far end of the dock. "The boat's been cleared for return to Mrs.

Collins, as is their car. Fingerprints were taken and the boat and car were photographed. Everything's been done and we're no closer to knowing what happened out on the water that night."

"What's the name of the boat?" Angie walked behind the chief. She hadn't paid any attention to the boat's name the day they'd found the grounded vessel.

No Place Like Home, the chief told her.

"I guess it didn't live up to its name." Courtney eyed the boat as they came up alongside it. With her hand on her hip, she let her eyes rove over the boat. "So what on earth happened on this thing?"

The chief climbed aboard and helped Ellie and Jenna from the dock to the vessel. Angie and Courtney each took one of Mr. Finch's arms to help steady him as they stepped onto the deck.

"Well, I can't remember the last time I was on a boat." Finch's eyes were wide taking it all in. "Maybe never."

"Really?" Courtney turned to the man. "You were never on a boat? You never even took a ferry?"

"I was in a rowboat once," Finch noted. He glanced at the cats as they sniffed out the new smells. "This must be something new for our fine felines, as well." Finch drew himself up. "I must focus on the task at hand. I mustn't let the new experience distract me. Something terrible happened here."

Angie stood off to the side and Courtney moved over next to her. "Do you feel it?"

Angie nodded. A humming seemed to run through the girls' veins pulsing out a rhythmic beat.

"My blood is humming, too." Courtney's expression was serious.

"How should we start?" Angie asked the chief.

Chief Martin cleared his throat. "So, it seems there was blood on the deck over here. And, here." He gestured to the rail. "Blood found in this area was indicative of a fight. We assume Ackerman and Collins fought in this section of the deck." The chief swiveled and pointed to the area. "The thought is that either Collins pushed Ackerman over the rail or perhaps Ackerman lost his balance and fell over during the fight. His body also showed an abdominal wound. From a knife."

"Tony Collins stabbed Ackerman?" Ellie looked faint.

Chief Martin gave a slight nod. "We assume it was Collins who stabbed him."

"What could have been the cause of the fight?" Jenna had a hand on Ellie's shoulder. "The two guys were business partners, weren't they?"

The chief nodded. "We've learned that the men were going to develop some land on Marion Island. Ackerman owned the property. He and Collins were to build luxury homes on the parcel. Collins had sunk a good deal of money into preparing the land and Ackerman wanted to back out of the deal.

It would have meant a huge loss for Mr. Collins's investment. It would take years in court fighting to get his money back. The whole mess could have ruined Collins financially."

"So he killed Ackerman in a rage?" Jenna shook her head.

"It seems that's what happened." The chief continued to share what he knew. "As you know, the weather took a turn for the worse right as the boat got underway. The wind was strong and the sea was rough." He stepped forward to the steps that led into the cabin. "This is where Deirdre claimed she and the baby were during the trip. Why don't you move around and see if you can pick up any clues." He tilted his head to the dock. "I'll wait over there out of the way." He stepped off the boat and settled into a director's chair placed on the dock.

The four sisters and Finch made eye contact and each one headed off to different places. The boat wasn't huge, but there were two decks and the cabin to investigate. Angie and Jenna went below, Mr. Finch moved to the railing where Ackerman probably went over into the sea, and Courtney and Ellie sat down on one of the cushioned seats on the deck.

In the cabin, Angie inspected the kitchen which led to a dining spot and a sitting room. Further back was a decent-sized bedroom and a bathroom. Jenna went into the bedroom to get a sense of where Deirdre claimed she was for most of the short journey. The covers on the double bed were askew. Some toys lay on the floor next to the bed. A few clothing items had been tossed on a chair in the corner.

In the sitting area, Angie saw a navy blue backpack on the small built-in sofa. She walked over and picked it up gingerly. The zipper was pulled and the sides of the bag sagged open. Angie pushed the opening wider and peered inside to see a tube of sunscreen, some sunglasses, and a pair of men's flip flops. She rustled her hand around inside to feel for anything else, but came up empty. She carried the backpack up to the deck and over to where the chief was sitting.

"Did you find the date rape drug that Louisa claimed to see in this backpack?"

"We didn't find anything like that." Chief Martin shielded his eyes from the sun. "That isn't to say drugs weren't on board. Collins could have thrown the vial into the ocean. He could have had it in his pocket. But, no, we didn't find anything."

Angie nodded, went below deck, and returned the backpack to the sofa. She shuffled around and then entered the bedroom to find Jenna sitting on the bed. "Anything?"

Jenna patted the mattress next to her. "Come sit for a minute."

Angie sat down. "Why do I feel exhausted?"

"I could come up with quite a few reasons."

Jenna pulled her long braid over her shoulder and ran her thumb and index finger over the tips of her hair. "There's something floating on the air down here."

Angie breathed slowly in and out several times. "I feel it, too. Something heavy, but not murderous. What does it mean?"

The two cats jumped up on the bed and gave the girls a start.

"How did you two get in here without us seeing you?" Jenna patted Circe's neck and Euclid pushed in between the two young women and sat.

"What do you cats think? Any ideas?" Angie ran her hand over Euclid's orange fur and closed her eyes. After a minute passed, she started to get flickers of images in her mind. Her heart rate picked up and Angie tried to slow things down by taking deeper breaths. Shadows passed in her vision. Someone stood in the kitchen. A sense of nervousness drifted in the air. She heard the fussing of a tired child. A medicinal smell tingled the airways of her nose. The boat rocked. Angie could feel red wine on her tongue.

Euclid let out a low growl and Angie's mind cleared. She took in a sharp breath and coughed.

Jenna rubbed her forehead and took a look at Angie. "Did you feel it?" She described the same things that Angie had just experienced.

"Did Tony drug Deirdre?" Angie rubbed Euclid's cheeks. "So he could kill Patrick Ackerman?"

"It seems like a strong possibility, doesn't it?" Jenna stood up slowly and stretched her back muscles. "Let's go get some air."

Angie and the cats followed Jenna up the stairs to the deck. Mr. Finch stood clutching the rail on the starboard side where the chief thought the fight had taken place.

Angie placed her hand on Finch's arm. "Do you feel anything?"

Mr. Finch ran his hand over the metal railing. "Chief Martin is correct. A fight took place here. The sea was rough. A man fell over this rail. His hand clutched the metal, right here on this spot, but it was wet and slippery and he couldn't hold on."

Angie's throat tightened. She squeezed Finch's arm.

"There's something else." The older man turned away from the rail. "I sense someone near the stairs and a man standing here." He pointed to a spot on deck about yard away. "I feel the boat lurch, and a man falling back against the railing." Finch narrowed his eyes and he sighed. "The sensation fades away and I can't see what happened next."

Jenna linked her arm though Finch's and they walked over to where Courtney sat with Ellie on the bench. Courtney had her arm around her sister.

"Did you sense anything?" Angie asked.

Courtney frowned. "I can feel that bad things happened here, but nothing is clear."

"That's because I've been blathering at her." Ellie clutched her hands together on her lap. "She hasn't had a quiet moment to think because I keep fussing at her."

Angie smiled. "You don't have to stay here, you know."

"Why don't you stroll over to the coffee shop?" Jenna gave Ellie's long blonde hair a playful tug. "No one wants you to be upset. Everyone understands."

Ellie's lips pursed and then she said, "I don't want to be such a baby. All of you can manage to be here without nearly passing out."

"I told Ellie I'd get off the boat with her, but she wouldn't budge." A long piece of honey colored hair slipped out of Courtney's loose bun and blew into her eyes. She pushed the strand away.

Ellie groaned. "I thought if I forced myself to stay, then I'd desensitize myself. I want to be able to help."

Angie looked sympathetically at her sister. "You don't have to torture yourself. You're always a help." She reached for Ellie's hand. "I've had enough of this boat. Let's go home."

CHAPTER 20

Angie sat at a café table in her bake shop laminating recipes for her smoothies and energy drinks so that they could be pinned above the counter where the blenders stood so that the new employees could easily access them. Jenna and Tom had gone to meet Betty at the house that Tom had recently put an offer on. He wanted Jenna to be sure about the house before he went forward with the purchase since it would be Jenna's home, too, now that they were engaged.

Courtney and Mr. Finch had returned to work at the candy store and Ellie had gone out to meet Jack Ford for coffee. The visit to the boat had left Ellie feeling drained so when Jack texted, she jumped at the chance see him. Angie knew her sister was always eager to be with Jack, but the Sweet Cove lawyer's invitation this afternoon was perfect timing since Ellie had been feeling low about not being able to help at the crime scene.

The cats were snoozing on top of the bake shop's new refrigerator. Angie glanced up at them and smiled. As she sipped her latte enjoying the unusual momentary quiet, she couldn't prevent her thoughts from drifting back to the boat, Tony Collins, Ackerman, and Deirdre. The things she'd learned floated around in her brain.

Patrick Ackerman and Tony had a business deal that soured which would have plunged Tony into financial difficulty or worse. Tony asked Louisa to meet him on Marion Island where she found the date rape drug in his backpack and figured out that he had a wife and a kid. On the late-night return trip to Sweet Cove, Tony and Ackerman fought and Ackerman went overboard. Tony Collins was missing.

Did Tony drug Deirdre to keep her from hearing his attack on Ackerman? Did Tony run away because he killed Ackerman? Or did Tony go over the rail and drown? Angie glanced out the window and a wave of nausea flooded her stomach. *Did Deirdre have something to do with Tony's disappearance? Is there a murderer staying in our carriage house apartment?*

A knock sounded on the bake shop door and Angie almost jumped out of her seat. Taking a deep breath, she saw Louisa peeking through the glass at her. Louisa waved and opened the door. "Hi. I can't wait to get started."

Angie stood up. She greeted her new employee and handed her a pale blue apron and a dark blue name tag with *Louisa* engraved on it. Louisa had come to the shop for her first afternoon of training.

Angie went over the recipes and the morning routine and showed the young woman the layout of the cabinets and what was stored in each one and then explained where the supplies were kept. Louisa practiced making several fruit smoothies, worked the machine that made the specialty drinks, and tried the new electronic cash register.

Two hours flew by with the cats keenly watching Louisa handle everything with energy and good cheer. When Louisa turned to Angie and asked what else she could do, the cats trilled their approval.

"That's about it." Angie smiled. "You're a real pro. It'll be great having you working here."

Louisa ran a cloth over all of the café tables. "Have you heard anything new on Tony Collins?"

Angie would have liked to share what they'd learned at the boat, but that was impossible without alerting Louisa to the sisters' paranormal skills. "Not much. Have you?"

"No." Louisa's face clouded and her black eyebrows scrunched together. "I haven't heard anything about Tony possessing the date rape drug. Maybe the media is keeping that quiet for some reason."

"That could be. Maybe the police don't want that information to get out." Angie couldn't tell her that the police hadn't found the drug on the boat. She wondered if Louisa was mistaken about discovering the sedative in Tony's backpack.

Louisa took off her apron and she and Angie agreed to meet one more time before the bake shop opened. Angie stepped onto the porch and waved as Louisa got into her car and backed out of the driveway. As she was turning to go back inside, she noticed Deirdre come out of the carriage house and go into the backyard. Angie removed her apron and tossed it on one of the chairs, and then she walked down the porch steps and into the rear garden.

Deirdre was sitting under the pergola in one of the Adirondack chairs. Her eyes were bloodshot and her facial skin looked loose and droopy. Angie thought she looked like she'd been drinking and when she got closer she could smell alcohol on the woman's breath.

"Is everything okay?" Angie took a seat opposite Deirdre who didn't look like she was happy for the company. Her auburn hair stuck up at angles like she'd just got up from a nap and when she ran her fingers over the top of her head, her hand trembled.

"Where's Brendan?" Angie asked.

Deirdre held up the receiver of a baby monitor. "He's taking a nap. I needed some air."

"Have you heard from Chief Martin?"

Deirdre gave a slight nod and gazed off to the flowerbeds that Ellie had worked so hard on. The garden was a riot of colorful blooms, but Deirdre didn't seem to notice. "I can take possession of the boat and the car tomorrow."

"That's great news." Angie tried to sound happy.

Deirdre forced the corners of her mouth to turn up, but she didn't speak.

Angie got a weird sensation from the young mother. She took a deep breath and tried to focus on her perception. She wanted to draw Deirdre into conversation before Brendan woke up and the opportunity passed.

"Have the police learned anything about what's happened to Tony?"

Deirdre's face hardened and she bit her lower lip. "No."

Angie decided to press for a reaction of some sort. "What was Tony like?"

Anger flushed Deirdre's cheeks and she glared at Angie. "He was a monster." Her tone sent a chill down Angie's back. "He ruined my life."

Angie swallowed hard and hoped her questions wouldn't send the woman fleeing into the carriage house. She sensed weakness in Deirdre's emotional state which had been helped along by too much drink and she felt badly about pushing her with questions, but the woman would leave the area soon and the chance to get information would disappear along with her.

"What happened?" Angie was careful to keep any hint of urgency out of her voice.

"What happened?" Deirdre's eyes flashed. She flattened her back against the chair and let out a whoosh of air. "Ha, what didn't happen?"

163

Angie waited. For a second it looked like Deirdre might close her eyes and doze off, but then she set her jaw and fiery words poured out of her mouth.

"He took everything from me. My friends. My home. He didn't care that I hated the boat. He controlled the money, gave me an allowance. I quit my job to travel with him. I felt cut off from people. He was so jealous." She let out a snort of disgust. "But he hooked up with women in every port." She shook her head. "He left me with nothing." Deidre's face softened for a second and she said softly, "Except Brendan."

Deirdre sat up so fast that Angie startled. The young woman narrowed her eyes and whispered. "I was sick of his emotional abuse. I was done with it." Suddenly, her face paled and her glassy eyes seemed to roll for a second. She gently placed her hand against her stomach. Angie thought that the alcohol Deirdre consumed must be playing havoc with her gut and wondered for a second if she might heave.

Deirdre took some long breaths. "I'm going in to check on Brendan." She pushed out of the chair, steadied herself, and walked to the carriage house.

"Are you going to be okay? Do you want me to sit with you?" Angie stood up.

Deirdre waved her hand dismissively without turning around.

"I'll be in the house," Angie called. "Just give me
164

a yell if you need something."

Deirdre disappeared inside the carriage house and slammed the door.

Angie stared after her. What had she said? How did she put it?

I was sick of his abuse. I was done with it.

Flickers of anxiety pulsed in Angie's veins.

CHAPTER 21

Ellie was in the kitchen starting dinner when Angie came in from the back door of the Victorian. When she saw Angie's face, Ellie stopped what she was doing. "What's wrong with you?"

"I just saw Deirdre in the yard." Angie related their conversation.

As she listened to her sister's interaction with Deirdre, Ellie's facial expression became more and more serious. "Oh, that *is* concerning." Her worry was making her squeeze the wooden spoon she was holding and when she realized how tightly she gripped the utensil she put it on the counter. "Deirdre clearly lays out a motive to get rid of Tony."

Angie sat at the center island and held her chin in her hand. "I don't know what to think. Would having a few drinks loosen Deirdre's tongue so much that she would risk giving me her motive for killing Tony? If she *is* a murderer, wouldn't she be more careful?"

"The stress of what she's done may be causing

her to make mistakes," Ellie said gravely. "You should tell Chief Martin."

"I will, but there isn't anything he can do without some evidence." Angie rubbed the back of her neck.

Ellie carried over a glass of iced tea. "Take a break from this stuff tonight. Let's make a nice dinner and relax. Maybe watch a movie later."

Angie sipped from her glass. "That's a great idea." She smiled at her sister, grateful for the suggestion to take the night off from the Collins situation. "Let's change the subject. How did your date with Jack go?"

Ellie's cheeks tinged pink and her eyes sparkled. "Very nice."

Angie chuckled. "You are clearly smitten with Mr. Ford."

Ellie winked and walked to the refrigerator, her long blonde hair swinging over her back. "And you are clearly correct."

Jenna walked into the room. "What's all this girlish giggling? It could only be about a man." She sat on the stool next to Angie and took a sip from her sister's glass of iced tea.

"I'm about to tease Ellie for mooning over Jack Ford." Angie slid her iced tea away from Jenna.

"Ooh." Jenna rubbed her hands together. "I'm in."

"Before you start in on me," Ellie said, "tell us about the house."

Jenna told her sisters about the house Tom had

made the offer on. "When we went to see it, Tom wanted to carry me over the threshold, but Betty grumped at us saying it would bring bad luck if he carried me prior to actually owning the place."

Ellie shook her head. "You should just ignore her."

"Well, I'm not superstitious, but I figured why court trouble." Jenna got up to make a salad. "The house is a disaster. I don't know how a place can fall into such disrepair. I was initially worried that Tom was biting off too much, but he's so enthusiastic and went on about all the renovations that he convinced me that it will be beautiful." She washed the lettuce in the sink. "I really like the idea of restoring the house to its former glory. I'm excited."

Ellie started to stir fry some chicken strips in the wok. "You know, you and Tom could always move into one of the carriage house apartments and live there if you want to get married before the house is finished."

"That's an idea." Jenna smiled as she pulled the big salad bowl from the lower cabinet. "If the house is going to take forever to complete, then maybe I'll suggest the carriage house to Tom and then we won't have to wait so long to get married."

"Right," Angie joked. "You don't want to be an old lady when you walk down the aisle."

"Look who's talking." Jenna chuckled as she gave it right back to her sister.

Angie ignored the comment. "I think I'll bake something for dessert." She headed to the cabinet that held the baking supplies.

"Make it something chocolate." Courtney walked in with Mr. Finch right behind her. "The candy store was nuts this afternoon. Does a full moon make people crave sugar?"

Mr. Finch filled the kettle with water and placed it on the burner. "We brought back some samples of a new fudge flavor." He opened the white box and placed the squares on a white plate. "After dinner, we would like your opinions."

The cats were resting on top of the fridge, but they sat up eagerly when they heard the talk about fudge.

Angie went over and sniffed the new confection. "Ah, heavenly."

As she extended her arm to take a square from the plate, Mr. Finch moved the platter out of her reach and scolded good-naturedly, "You'll have to wait until *after* dinner to taste-test, Miss Angie."

Angie mock pouted as she returned to the baking cabinet. "What about a chocolate mousse pie for dessert?"

"Yes, please," Courtney said, her face lighting up. "We haven't had that for ages."

Angie bent to get the pie plate she wanted to use, but couldn't find it in the lower cabinet. She checked two other cabinets before it occurred to her where it might be. "I think I left the deep dish pie

169

plate in the carriage house apartment when Mr. Finch was staying there." Her face clouded. "I guess I'll have to go get it."

Ellie turned, knowing that Angie's reluctance stemmed from the recent conversation with Deirdre. "You want me to do it?"

Angie sighed and started for the back door. "I'll go. I should probably check on Deirdre and make sure she hasn't passed out."

The others looked at Angie with concern. "What's going on?" Courtney asked.

"Ellie will tell you." Angie stepped out the back door and made her way to the carriage house. She climbed the stairs to the second floor and knocked on the apartment door, dread skittering over her skin.

Deirdre pulled the door open with a jerk and glared at Angie. "Yes?"

Angie thought that Deirdre should probably use more tact since she was being allowed to stay for free in the Roseland sisters' place. "I left a pie plate in here. If you don't mind, I'd like to get it."

Deirdre looked like she might decline Angie's request. She took a quick glance over her shoulder, then gave a slight nod and stepped back to let Angie enter. "I'm just making some dinner for Brendan." The little boy was sitting on the living area floor playing with a ball and some blocks.

Angie hurried into the kitchen and looked through two of the cabinets before she found what she wanted. "Here it is." She walked briskly to the door carrying the pie plate in a hurry to get out of the apartment. As she reached for the doorknob, Brendan babbled at her, pushed the ball and let it roll towards Angie. She picked it up and took a few steps closer to the little boy. She rolled the ball gently to him. "Here's the ball, Brendan."

He opened his little hand and the ball bumped his fingers. Brendan squealed with delight. Angie smiled and as she turned to leave, she noticed a tan backpack on the floor near the sofa. The back of her neck tingled like tiny needles pricking her skin.

"Thanks," Angie told Deirdre as she went out the door. She hustled down the stairs, across the lawn, and into the Victorian.

Courtney saw the pie plate in Angie's hand. "Thank heavens you found it. I was afraid we wouldn't be able to have the mousse pie."

"I need to make a phone call." Angie put the pie plate on the counter and reached for her phone. She pressed in some numbers.

"Now what?" Ellie asked.

Angie raised her index finger to indicate that she'd tell her in a minute. When no one answered and voicemail came on, Angie said, "Louisa, it's Angie. Would you give me a call when you get this?"

"What's going on?" Jenna came over to stand beside her sister.

Angie brushed her hair back from her face.

171

"Remember Louisa said she saw a vial of sedative in Tony's backpack when she was on the boat? How did she know it was *Tony's* backpack?" Angie looked pointedly at her sisters and Mr. Finch. "There's a backpack upstairs in the carriage house apartment."

Mr. Finch leaned on the island counter. "Are you thinking, Miss Angie, that the sedative was in Mrs. Collins's backpack, not Tony's?"

"It's possible, isn't it?" Angie asked.

"Deirdre had the sedative." Ellie's eyes widened at the revelation. "She gave it to Tony so it would be easier to push him overboard."

"She told you she'd had enough of him," Courtney noted. "Ellie told us what Deirdre said to you in the yard." She tilted her head. "You think she killed her husband?"

Angie lifted her hands palm side up. "She did have motive."

"And opportunity," Jenna added.

They all stared at each other pondering the possibility that Deirdre may be a murderer when Angie's phone buzzed.

Ellie said, "It must be Louisa."

Angie's brow furrowed when she saw who was calling. She answered and listened for a minute. "Okay. I'll be there soon." She clicked off. "It was Aunt Anna. Chief Martin told her our suspicions about Jacob being responsible for putting the beds in her barn. She said she wanted to confront him about it."

"What did he say when she spoke with him?" Finch asked.

"Nothing. He hasn't shown up to work in her yard for two days."

"He must know we're on to him, so he took off." Courtney frowned.

Angie's voice trembled. "There's more. Anna said she found something in the barn that isn't hers. She wants us to see it."

"Right now?" Jenna asked.

Angie nodded.

"So much for that mousse pie," Courtney sighed.

CHAPTER 22

Since they were in the middle of cooking dinner, Ellie offered to stay at home to finish making the meal. She would put the food in the refrigerator and heat it up when her sisters returned. The girls thought that Mr. Finch should skip the visit to Anna's house since he had just worked a full shift at the candy store. They didn't want him to overdo and although he protested about not going along, Finch agreed that he was tired and decided to head to his house for a nap. He would return to the Victorian when the sisters arrived home and then they would all gather for dinner to hear what Anna had discovered in her barn.

The girls gathered their things, left the house, and headed to Jenna's car. Circe followed Mr. Finch into the car and Jenna drove around the block to let him out at his place. Finch and the black cat headed to the front door, where the man turned and waved as the car drove away.

On the short drive to Anna's house, Jenna, Courtney, and Angie tried to figure out what Anna had found in the barn and speculated about what might cause Jacob's absence outside of being guilty of placing beds in the barn. They couldn't come up with any idea that would explain why Jacob didn't tell Anna that he would not be around to work the past two days.

As Jenna pulled into the dark driveway and parked, Anna came out of the house and waved to them from the porch. "Come in." She thanked the girls for coming to see her so quickly. "Part of me worries that something has happened to Jacob and the other part of me suspects he *did* hide those things in my barn. Honestly, I don't know what to think."

"You called Chief Martin?" Angie asked.

Anna nodded. "He'll be here soon." She led the girls into her cozy living room. "That's what I found in the barn." She pointed to a metal strong box that she had placed on the coffee table. "After I heard that Jacob might be the guilty party, I decided to look around inside the barn. I didn't go up to the hayloft, of course, but I took a pitch fork and poked around in some old hay bales on the first floor. I came up empty, so I walked around checking out nooks and crannies and found this tucked along some of the wooden studs of the wall."

"When did you find it? Angie asked.

"The very night you were here last." Anna's lips were thin and tight.

"Maybe that's why Jacob hasn't been seen the

past two days." Jenna wondered if Jacob had discovered that his metal container was missing and took off.

"You haven't opened the box?" Courtney leaned down to look it over.

"No. I thought it best to have others here with me." Anna sat on the soft sofa. "I hope it isn't a bomb."

Jenna looked wide-eyed at Anna. She hadn't thought of that possibility.

Anna's house phone rang and she reached for the phone on the side table. When she clicked off, she said, "Phillip is running late. He stopped at Jacob's apartment. No one answered his knock. He looked in the windows, but from what he can see, everything looks in order. Jacob's van is in the driveway."

"Maybe he hasn't taken off then." Angie breathed a sigh of relief despite the hums of anxiety flitting in her veins. "He could have gone away with a friend for a couple of days," she added hopefully.

"Wouldn't he have told Anna that he wouldn't be around if he was taking a couple of days off?" Jenna asked.

"I guess." Angie's voice was small.

"Phillip said to go ahead and open the box." Anna eyed the metal case. "He has to answer another police call before he can get here. He said if there's anything inside the box then we should use gloves or a tissue to lift out whatever is in there.

176

We don't want to leave fingerprints. He said you girls know what to do."

The three sisters nodded and eyed each other. "Anyone want to do the honors?" Jenna questioned.

"I will." Courtney knelt beside the coffee table. "There isn't a lock on it?"

"No. It seems you can just lift the lid," Anna observed. She looked nervously at the container. "I thought whoever put the food and the beds in the loft might hide something else in the barn. I thought it was logical to assume that the person wouldn't put everything in one place, so I decided to poke around the first floor of the barn. And, lo and behold." Anna gestured to the box. "I found something that is not mine."

"Ready?" Courtney put her hands on the metal container. She glanced at her sisters and at Anna. "Here we go." She pushed the lid up and back.

Four heads bent to see.

Inside were a stack of documents. Angie took a few tissues from her purse and wrapped them around her fingers. She reached in, removed some of the items, and put them on the table. Courtney used the eraser end of a pencil to move the things around. "This is Jacob's picture on this license, but the name is Derrick Rivers." She looked up with a questioning expression. There was a passport and a credit card in the same name.

Angie carefully pushed the front cover open on another passport and she let out a gasp. "It's

Deirdre." The sisters leaned closer to see.

"But it's a different name." Jenna read aloud. "Linda Harding." She blinked. "What's going on? Which are the real names?"

Angie lifted some other things from the box. "Here's a credit card and driver's license for Linda Harding. And here's a birth certificate for Robert Harding. This must be for Brendan." She let out a long low sigh. "Jacob and Deirdre must have arranged these false documents. They're planning to disappear."

Anna sucked in a breath and put her hand on her chest. "Oh, my. Those two know each other? Did Jacob arrange for that boat to get grounded near my property?" Color rose in Anna's face. "He was the one who alerted us to the grounded boat." The older woman shook her head in disgust.

"The beds must have been for Deirdre and Brendan." Courtney stood up. "Jacob must have planned for them to stay for a night or two and then take off with the new identification."

"Why wouldn't they have just taken off right away? Why stay around?" Jenna's forehead creased as she pondered the reason.

Anna's mouth dropped open for a moment and then she spoke, her voice almost a whisper. "Jacob and that woman arranged to kill the husband so they could take off together." Her fingers trembled as she passed her hand over her face.

Angie's throat tightened. "Maybe they wanted to

hide Deirdre and Brendan for a while. So the police would think she and the baby had fallen overboard, too. Maybe Deirdre wanted to wait until Tony's body washed up to be sure he was dead."

Angie's phone buzzed and she stood up to answer the call. She stepped onto the porch and after a couple of minutes, she returned to the living room. Her eyes were wide.

"Was it Louisa?" Jenna walked over to her sister.

Angie gave a slight nod. "Louisa said the backpack was either tan or light brown. I asked her if there was anything else in the pack. She said there was a fleece sweatshirt inside. Green. With the words *Columbia University* written on the front." Angie's eyes flashed. "That's Deirdre's sweatshirt. Deirdre's backpack is tan. *Deirdre* had the sedative in her backpack, not Tony."

Jenna's lips turned down. "Deirdre must have used the sedative on Tony, and then she pushed him off the boat right after Tony fought with Ackerman. She killed him."

Angie thought about Deirdre's words when they spoke in the garden. *Tony is a monster. He took everything from me.* Her heart sank. "Deirdre could only think of one way out of the marriage and that was to kill her husband."

"She and Jacob must be in love. They must be going to run away together." Courtney's eyes went wide and her tone was urgent. "Call Chief Martin.

Deirdre has her car now. She just got it back from the police today. She must have been waiting for dark. She's going to get away."

Jenna grabbed her car keys from the table. "Maybe Jacob is with her. We need to go home. Call Ellie. Tell her to watch Deirdre's car."

The girls rushed from Anna's house.

"Good luck," Anna called after them. "Be careful!"

CHAPTER 23

Ellie's heart pounded like a drum. She clicked off from Courtney and edged to the window overlooking the driveway. Pressing her body against the wall, she slowly leaned her head forward. The floodlight on the side of the carriage house lit up the spot in front of the building where Deirdre's car was parked. It was still there. There didn't seem to be any movement around it. *Why am I here alone? Where are the cats?* Ellie took a quick look at the top of the fridge and remembered that Circe went with Mr. Finch to his house. *But where was Euclid?* She called the orange cat's name, but he was nowhere to be seen. *Where is Chief Martin?*

Ellie moved to the back hall near the door to the yard and peeked out. She didn't see anyone around, so she unlocked the door and stepped down the granite steps into the garden. When she went outside, Ellie would normally take in a deep breath to smell the sweet blooming flowers, but tonight she didn't even notice the fragrance. She moved her gaze to the windows of the second floor apartment. The lights were off and the place was in darkness. *Maybe Deirdre and the baby went to bed early.* She made a face. *Or they've escaped. But, how? Her car is still here.*

Ellie stood still trying to pick up on any noises. The night sounds of cicadas and tree crickets calling out to their mates made the air buzz and hum. Ellie's eyes adjusted to the dark and she noticed that the door to the carriage house was open a crack. Her heart jumped into her throat when she thought she heard a creak on the steps. She froze. *Someone was coming down the carriage house steps.*

Ellie stood stock still. She didn't know where the person was on the staircase so she didn't know if she had time to creep back into the house or if standing completely still in the darkness was the best way not to be detected.

Something rustled in the tree line at the rear of the property. Ellie held her breath and squinted trying to see what was making the sounds. Euclid stepped out of the shadows and into a patch of moonlight. He walked towards the Victorian.

Just as someone stepped out the carriage house, Euclid made eye contact with Ellie. In order to draw the person's attention away from Ellie, the big orange cat arched his back and let out a howl. Deirdre let out a yelp of surprise at the animal. She had Brendan in her arms and had her backpack flung over her shoulder.

Euclid, with his back still arched, hissed menacingly at the woman showing his sharp, pointy teeth. He moved forward slowly, his back still arched, his ears pinned to his head.

Deirdre took halting steps to Euclid's left trying to get around him. Ellie could tell that Deirdre wanted to get to the walkway that led from the Roseland's backyard to Finch's rear lawn through the grove of trees at the property line. *She must be meeting Jacob over on Mr. Finch's street.*

Ellie moved into the shadow of the house trying to decide what to do.

Deirdre swung her backpack at Euclid. "Go away," she growled at the cat. She broke into a trot, but Euclid's hissing grew louder and he began a series of attacks on Deirdre's legs. The huge cat darted in, bit, and zoomed away, over and over he kept up his offensive, striking and rushing away only to return for the next assault.

Ellie's phone vibrated in her pocket with a text from Mr. Finch. *There is a white van idling in front of my house. I'm suspicious.*

The air was filled with Deirdre's shouting, Euclid's hissing, and Brendan's fussing. Deirdre started to run and Euclid pursued her.

Ellie took off after them. She ran along the new walkway between the yards pushing past the low hanging tree limbs to emerge onto Finch's back lawn where she saw Jacob running from the street to Deirdre's side. Jacob grabbed Brendan from Deirdre and he raced towards his white van still idling at the curb.

When Jacob pulled open the driver's side door, Circe was sitting in the driver's seat. She hissed and batted at the young man, rearing back on her hind legs.

Ellie caught up to Deirdre and lunged, tackling her and taking her down, with the two of them landing hard on the lawn in a tangled pile.

Mr. Finch sat in the front passenger seat of the van. He turned his head and leaned over the middle console. "Going somewhere?" he asked Jacob.

Jacob's eyes darted around trying to figure out what to do just as a police car hurtled down the street and swerved to block the van from moving. Chief Martin got out and strode to where Jacob stood holding Brendan who was now wailing at the top of his lungs. A second police car jerked to a stop behind the chief's vehicle and two officers jumped out and ran over to Jacob and the baby.

As one officer cuffed Jacob and the other one took Brendan in his arms, Chief Martin hurried to the two women still prone on the grass. He couldn't help but smirk when he saw Ellie extricate herself from Deirdre and stand up, her clothes disheveled and her hair sticking out in wild disarray. "Nice work," he grinned. The chief extended his hand to Deirdre and helped her to her feet.

Deirdre ranted about a crazy cat and the blonde witch who tackled her.

Ellie brushed at her clothes to remove the dirt and blades of grass. She muttered to Deirdre, "Tell it to the judge."

Deirdre glared at the officer who had a grip on Jacob's arm. "Get your hands off my brother," she shrieked.

Brother? Ellie stared at her.

Courtney, Jenna, and Angie came running from the backyard of the Victorian and up to Mr. Finch's front lawn. They were out of breath from their sprint and their eyes were wide as they looked from Ellie to Deirdre to Jacob and the officers. Finch leaned over from inside the van and waved to the girls. Circe trilled from the driver's seat and Euclid sat on the lawn licking his mussed fur.

Courtney's shoulders drooped. "We missed it," she said dejectedly.

CHAPTER 24

Mr. Finch stood on the porch holding a silver tray containing tiny carrot cake cupcakes wrapped in individual pale blue bags tied with navy ribbons. Since the cats weren't allowed inside, they sat on the new bench that stood next to the bake shop door. The new "Sweet Dreams Bake Shop" sign hung over the entrance and a line of people snaked down the porch steps and around the house nearly to the sidewalk.

A huge flag with the words "Grand Opening" on it flew from the flag pole at the front of the Victorian. Rufus Fudge and Courtney walked along the line carrying trays with small complimentary cups of different flavored iced lattes for the people waiting to get in. Clusters of blue and pink balloons were tied to the porch rails and a bluegrass trio played happy, energetic music. Some people sat on the lawn of the Victorian soaking up the cheerful atmosphere, nibbling on treats and sipping coffees, teas, and specialty drinks. The sounds of laughter and happy chatter filled the air.

Inside the new bake shop, pleasant chaos ensued with orders being taken and filled as fast as Angie, Jenna, Ellie, Louisa, and two other new employees could manage. All of Angie's regular customers arrived to see the new bake shop. Much praise was heaped on Tom for his beautiful work. People called out congratulations to Angie while others told her how happy they were that the new place had finally opened.

"It seems a long time coming," Angie agreed.

Aunt Anna and Francine from the stained glass studio entered the store and beamed at Angie. Jenna wiped down a table that had just been vacated and waved the women over.

"What fun." Francine smiled. "I love it. I must make a habit of coming down here some mornings for coffee." She and Anna decided to arrange a twice a week morning gathering with their friends and acquaintances at the new bake shop.

"We could use a change of venue," Anna said. "It keeps things interesting."

Bessie and her husband from the Pirate's Den restaurant in the center of town sat at a table by the windows with Chief Martin and Officer Landers. The chief got up and hugged his aunt when she came in. Mildred and Agnes Walsh who used to work at the candy store when Mr. Finch's brother owned it stood gossiping in the corner with some town employees.

Angie stepped out from behind the counter when

Denise Landers came into the bake shop with her ninety-year-old mother Flora Walters who held tight to her daughter's arm. Angie hugged them and led the women to a table at the front of the room. "You don't have your wheelchair today? Tom put in the ramp at the end of the porch to accommodate anyone who might have trouble with steps."

"My dear girl," Mrs. Walters said. "I wanted to enter your lovely new shop today on my own two feet." She winked. "The wheelchair is out by the driveway."

"I saved some chocolate cupcakes for you," Angie smiled.

Mrs. Walters clapped her hands together. "My favorite."

Louisa took their drink orders and Angie went to get the cupcakes. Before they knew it, it was three in the afternoon, the bake shop door was locked and the bustle was over, ending a successful grand opening. Angie, beaming with joy, thanked everyone for their help and collapsed in one of the café chairs for a few moments before heading inside to shower. In two hours, the family was being treated to a tour of Tom and Jenna's new house.

***

JACK FORD sat next to Ellie on the sofa in the Victorian's living room holding her hand. Ellie's face was bright and her eyes were sparkling. The sisters were telling Jack the details of what had happened with the Collins case.

"You're amazing," Jack told Ellie. He looked as proud as a peacock gazing at his girlfriend. "You're very brave."

Ellie was soaking up his praise. "Well, I did my best to stop them, but I think the cats and Mr. Finch are much braver than I am." Her smile faded a bit. "In fact, I'm not brave at all."

Courtney sat on the floor next to the cats. "You don't give yourself enough credit, Sis. You need to be more like Euclid. He knows who he is and he's proud of it."

Euclid flicked his plume in the air and then curled the huge tail around his front paws. He trilled at Ellie.

Angie was quiet sitting next to Mr. Finch. She breathed a heavy sigh. "The four of you were great. You kept them from getting away."

"You don't sound happy about it, Miss Angie." Finch looked over his glasses at her. Angie could see that Mr. Finch felt the same way she did.

"The whole thing is a huge mess." Angie shook her head. "Tony Collins was a horrible person. He controlled Deirdre. He intimidated her. I understand why she did what she did. And I understand why Jacob did what he did."

Jenna agreed. "I'd do the same for any of you."

Deirdre planned to escape from Tony's tyranny

by drugging him and manning the boat to a secluded slip of beach in Silver Cove. Jacob was going to meet them there and take them to Anna's barn for a couple of days. The hope was that the authorities would believe that Deirdre and her son had fallen overboard. Jacob and Deirdre wanted to wait to take off because they didn't want Deirdre and Brendan to be recognized on the road. Jacob got the fake IDs and hid the beds in Anna's barn. He was the one who was skulking around at the studio apartment. He was trying to find Deirdre.

Angie said, "Deirdre put the sedative in a glass of wine and carried two glasses up to the deck. Ackerman arrived and Tony asked Deirdre to go below and get a beer for the guest. When she returned with it, she didn't know which glass of wine had the drug in it. Tony had a glass in his hand and told Deirdre to join them in a toast. Turned out, she had the drugged wine."

Jenna continued the story. "Deirdre went below. She passed out. The fight between Tony and Ackerman roused her and she dragged herself up to the deck. Deirdre collapsed at the top of the stairs. She saw Tony stab Ackerman who stumbled back and fell over the railing. Tony saw that Deirdre witnessed the whole thing. He started towards her with the knife, but the boat lurched, and Tony fell against the rails. Deirdre passed out. She wasn't sure if Tony went over the rail or not."

Courtney told more of what happened. "She was

afraid Tony was alive, hiding out because he killed Ackerman. She was terrified that he would come to kill her because she'd witnessed it."

Ellie rubbed her forehead. "Deirdre lost the over the counter phone she was using to communicate with Jacob when she was on the boat. She had no way to contact him. After hours of the boat moving in circles, Deirdre tried to take the helm, but she could barely keep conscious. The best she could do was to beach the vessel near Aunt Anna's house. Her brother was frantic that night trying to find where the boat had landed. When he saw it at the bottom of the bluff the next morning, he had to pretend that he didn't know Deirdre."

The day after the police took Deirdre and her brother into custody, Tony Collins' body washed ashore about five miles south of Sweet Cove.

Angie let out a sigh. "Deirdre can finally rest now that Tony's body has been found. She doesn't have to be afraid that he's alive and will come after her someday."

"What a mess." Courtney ran her hand over Euclid's soft fur. "But like you said, I would have done it for any of you or for my child to get him away from Tony and his emotional abuse."

"What will happen to Deirdre and her brother?" Ellie asked. "They didn't kill anyone and never intended to. They just wanted to drug Tony so that Deirdre and Brendan could escape from him."

"There will probably be minor charges filed for

possession of the sedative." Angie leaned back against the sofa. "Aunt Anna could file charges against Jacob for trespass or something, but she told Chief Martin that she would not pursue that. She's just glad that it's settled and she feels safe again in her home."

Betty Hayes flew into the foyer from the front porch. "Did I hear the word home?" She bustled over to Mr. Finch and gave him a big kiss. "Such a handsome man," Betty cooed. "How did I ever get so lucky?"

Finch blushed and squeezed her hand.

"Who's ready to see Tom and Jenna's new house?" Betty jangled the keys. Tom had just closed on the house two doors down from the Victorian and he and Jenna were eager to show the family the place that would eventually be their new home.

Jenna stood up. "Tom's running late. He's going to meet us there."

Everyone, including the cats, filed out of the house and turned left onto the sidewalk. Jenna looked back at the Victorian with a wistful expression. "You know, it will be strange leaving the Victorian and all of you and moving into my own house someday." She looked at Mr. Finch. "It must have been hard leaving Chicago and moving here. You'd lived in Chicago your whole life."

Finch, Angie, and Jenna stood on the sidewalk gazing at the beautiful Victorian house. "It really wasn't hard to move here, Miss Jenna. Home isn't just a house or a town or a city. We carry home in our hearts and we can take it with us wherever we go."

Jenna's eyes got misty. She wrapped Mr. Finch in a tight bear hug which knocked him slightly off balance for a second and she had to grip his arm to steady him. They chuckled. Jenna put her hand on Finch's shoulder. "I don't know what we'd do without you, Mr. Finch." She kissed him gently on the cheek.

Jenna and Angie hooked their arms through Mr. Finch's and they headed to catch up with the others. Everyone was on the porch of the house by the time they turned onto the walkway that led to the front door. Tom had the keys in his hand and he gave Jenna a sweet kiss. He put the key in the lock and pushed the door open. Everyone cheered.

"Home sweet home," Tom said to Jenna. He grinned. "Someday, anyway."

Betty cleared her throat. "Now that you two own the house, Tom, you may carry Jenna over the threshold."

Tom looked tenderly at the lovely brunette standing next to him. "If it's okay with Jenna, I'd prefer we enter side by side, and hand in hand. Partners, best friends, and...." Tom leaned close to Jenna's ear and whispered, "lovers."

The cats trilled.

Jenna smiled up at Tom and took his hand and

they led the way into their new home with their
family and friends and two fine felines right behind
them.

THANK YOU FOR READING!

BOOKS BY J.A. WHITING CAN BE FOUND HERE:

www.amazon.com/author/jawhiting

To hear about new books and book sales, please sign up for my mailing list at:

www.jawhitingbooks.com

Your email will never be sold, shared, or spammed.

SWEET COVE COZY MYSTERIES

The Sweet Dreams Bake Shop (Sweet Cove Cozy Mystery Book 1)
Murder So Sweet (Sweet Cove Cozy Mystery Book 2)
Sweet Secrets (Sweet Cove Cozy Mystery Book 3)
Sweet Deceit (Sweet Cove Cozy Mystery Book 4)
Sweetness and Light (Sweet Cove Cozy Mystery

Book 5)
Home Sweet Home (Sweet Cove Cozy Mystery Book 6)

And more to come!

LIN COFFIN COZY MYSTERIES

A Haunted Murder (A Lin Coffin Cozy Mystery Book 1)
A Haunted Disappearance (A Lin Coffin Cozy Mystery Book 2) – Soon!

And more to come!

MYSTERIES

The Killings (Olivia Miller Mystery – Book 1)
Red Julie (Olivia Miller Mystery - Book 2)
The Stone of Sadness (Olivia Miller Mystery - Book 3)

And more to come!

If you enjoyed the book, please consider leaving a review.

A few words are all that's needed.

It would be very much appreciated.

ABOUT THE AUTHOR

J.A. Whiting lives with her family in New England where she works full time in education. Whiting loves reading and writing mystery and suspense stories.

VISIT ME AT:

www.jawhitingbooks.com

www.facebook.com/jawhitingauthor

www.amazon.com/author/jawhiting

SOME RECIPES FROM THE SWEET COVE SERIES

CHEWY CHOCOLATE CHIP BARS

Ingredients

*1½ sticks unsalted butter (nicely softened)
*⅓ cup sugar
*1 cup light brown sugar
*1 large egg, with an additional large egg yolk
*2¼ teaspoons vanilla extract
*2¼ cups unbleached All-Purpose Flour
*½ teaspoon baking soda
*½ teaspoon salt
*2 cups chocolate chips (you may use white, semi-sweet, dark, milk, or peanut butter flavor – or mix different flavors together)

Directions

*Preheat the oven to 350 degrees.

*Grease and flour a 9 or 13 inch pan (or line the pan with foil leaving a bit hanging over the edges and spray with non-stick spray – you can lift the bars from the pan by grasping the ends of the foil).

*In a separate bowl, mix together the flour, baking soda and salt.

*Cream together the butter, sugar, brown sugar, and vanilla.

*Beat the egg and the extra egg yolk into the butter mixture.

*Slowly beat the flour mixture into the butter mixture.

*With a rubber spatula, stir in the chips of your choice.

*Spread the mixture into the 9 X 13 inch pan.

*Bake in a preheated 375°F oven for 20 to 25 minutes until the top is golden and is slightly firm to the touch.

*Cool on a wire rack and then cut into 2 inch bars.

ROASTED TOMATO-BASIL SOUP

Ingredients

*3 pounds ripe plum tomatoes cut in half
*¼ cup plus 2 tablespoons of olive oil
*1 tablespoon salt
*1½ teaspoons ground black pepper
*2 cups chopped yellow onions (2 onions)
*5 garlic cloves, minced
*2 tablespoons unsalted butter
*¼ teaspoon crushed red pepper flakes
*1 (28-ounce) can of plum tomatoes and the juice from the can
*2 cups fresh basil leaves
*1 teaspoon fresh thyme leaves
*1 quart vegetable stock

Directions

*Preheat the oven to 400 degrees F.

*Mix together tomatoes, ¼ cup olive oil, salt, and pepper.

*Spread the tomato mixture on a baking sheet; roast for 40 minutes.

*In an 8-10 quart pot sauté the onions and garlic with 2 tablespoons of olive oil, the butter, and red pepper flakes over medium heat until the onions start to brown.

*Add the canned tomatoes, basil, thyme, and vegetable stock.

*Add the oven-roasted tomatoes. Also add the liquid from the baking sheet.

*Bring to a boil and simmer uncovered for 40 minutes.

*Pour into a blender or a food processor and smooth to preference.

*Note: This soup can be served hot or cold.

MASCARPONE DIP

Ingredients

*2 containers of mascarpone
*4 teaspoons of vanilla or kahlua
*4-6 tablespoons of powdered sugar
*¼ cup of cream (may substitute milk)
*Chocolate chips to taste (if desired)

Directions

*Empty containers of mascarpone into a bowl and whisk to smooth.

*Whisk in powdered sugar, vanilla (or kahlua), and cream (or milk) until smooth.

*Add chocolate chips (if desired) and blend into the mixture.

*Spoon into a serving dish.

*Use as a topping for berries or serve with the cannoli cookies (next recipe).

CANNOLI COOKIES

Ingredients

*2 cups all-purpose flour
*½ teaspoon baking soda
*½ teaspoon salt
*½ cup unsalted butter, softened
*⅓ cup whole-milk ricotta
*1 cup granulated sugar
*1 teaspoon pure vanilla extract
*1 large egg
*Powdered sugar to sprinkle over the cookies

Directions

*Preheat the oven to 350 degrees F.

*In a medium bowl, whisk the flour, baking soda, and salt until well combined.

*Beat the butter and ricotta on medium-high speed until light and fluffy, about 2 minutes.

*Add the sugar and vanilla; beat until blended, about 3 minutes.

*On medium speed, add the egg and beat until mixed.

*Add the flour mixture and mix on low speed until blended.

*Scrape the dough from the sides of the bowl, cover the bowl with plastic, and refrigerate for about 30 minutes.

*Line baking sheets with nonstick parchment.

*Drop the batter using tablespoons 2 inches apart on the baking sheets.

*Bake until the cookies are lightly golden, about 15 minutes.

*Let the cookies cool on the sheets for 5 minutes before transferring them to wire racks to cool completely.

Sprinkle with powdered sugar.

*May be served with the mascarpone dip (previous recipe).

*Note: You can store the cookies at room temperature or freeze in an airtight container (separate the cookie layers with waxed paper).

ANGIE'S CHOCOLATE MOUSSE PIE

Ingredients - Pie Crust

You may use your favorite pie crust recipe, a store-bought crust, or the chocolate crust recipe below.

Ingredients - Chocolate Pie Crust

*24 chocolate sandwich cookies (such as Oreos) or 24 chocolate cookie wafers
*½ stick unsalted butter, cut into pieces and softened

Ingredients - Chocolate Mousse

*2 cups of semisweet chocolate morsels
*2 cups of cold heavy cream
*2 teaspoons of powdered sugar
*1 teaspoon of vanilla extract

Ingredients – Whipped Topping (if desired)

*1 tablespoon of powdered sugar
*1 teaspoon of vanilla extract
*1½ cups of cold heavy cream

Directions – Chocolate Cookie Crust

*Heat the oven to 350°F and place the rack in the middle of the oven.

Food Processor Method

*Place the cookies in a food processor with a blade attachment. Process until the pieces are about the size of peas.

*Stop the processor, add the softened butter, and continue to process until the crumbs are fine, about the size of coarse, ground coffee (you will need 1½ cups).

Or, Rolling Pin Method

If you don't have a food processor, place the cookies in a re-sealable plastic bag, press out the air, and close tightly. Using a rolling pin, crush into uniform fine crumbs. Transfer to a medium bowl, add the softened butter, and mix until evenly combined.

*Pour the crumb mixture into a 9-inch pie plate. Use the bottom of a cup or your fingers and press the mixture firmly and evenly into the bottom of the pie plate and up the sides. Bake about 10 to 15 minutes.

*Remove to a wire rack to cool completely (about 30 minutes).

Directions – Chocolate Mousse

*Place 2 cups of morsels and ¾ cup of cream in a sauce pan.

*Melt the chocolate over medium heat, stirring occasionally with a wire whisk until the mixture is smooth and combined with the cream.

*Remove from the heat.

*Place the remaining 1¼ cups of cream, powdered sugar, and vanilla into a bowl and beat on high speed until stiff peaks form, about 1 minute.

*Using a spatula, slowly fold 2 cups of whipped cream into the melted chocolate. Try not to deflate the whipped cream.

*Spoon the mousse into the cooled pie crust and smooth to make an even layer. Chill in the refrigerator until set, about 2-3 hours.

*To serve: Top with whipped cream if desired (recipe below) and grate some chocolate shavings from a chocolate bar over the top of the pie.

Directions – Whipped Cream Topping

*Place 1¼ cups of cream, powdered sugar, and vanilla into a bowl and beat on high speed until stiff peaks form (about 1 minute).

*Top the pie with the cream.

ANGIE'S CARROT CAKE

Ingredients

*2 cups all-purpose flour
*1½ teaspoons baking soda
*1 teaspoon of baking powder
*2 teaspoons of cinnamon
*½ teaspoon of ginger
*½ teaspoon salt
*1 cup canola oil
*1 cup sugar
*4 eggs
*3 cups grated carrots

Directions

*Preheat the oven to 350 degrees.

*Mix the flour, baking soda, baking powder, cinnamon, ginger, and salt together until well-combined.

*Beat the eggs with a wire whisk and then add the oil and sugar and combine well.

*Add the egg mixture to the flour mixture and stir well to combine.

*Add the grated carrots and stir well to blend.

*Bake in a greased and floured bundt pan or two 9 inch round pans for about 40 minutes or until a toothpick comes out clean (or with just a few moist crumbs attached).

*Cool completely before frosting.

*Frost with your favorite cream cheese frosting or sprinkle with confectioner's sugar; if using the two round pans, frost one layer, top with the second layer, and frost.

ENJOY!

50253881R00132

Made in the USA
Lexington, KY
09 March 2016